NATALIE OPHELIA RHODES

Wild Quarter Mile

First edition

This book was professionally typeset on Reedsy.
Find out more at reedsy.com

To everyone who's ever loved someone with fire in their soul and scars on their heart.
To the girls who waited for the right one, and the boys who never thought they were enough.
For those who believe in second chances, slow burns, and wild rides—
And to the "friend" who tried to keep me from finishing this book: You failed. I finished it anyway.

Contents

⚠ Content Warning

Wild Quarter Mile is a steamy contemporary romance featuring emotionally intense themes and mature content. Reader discretion is advised. This story includes:

Explicit Sexual Content: Multiple graphic sex scenes, including light power exchange, public teasing, and dirty talk.

Strong Language: Frequent use of profanity and adult language.

Alcohol Use: Characters consume alcohol recreationally and socially, sometimes to cope with stress.

Toxic Family Dynamics: Depictions of emotional neglect, resentment in long-term parental relationships, and verbal tension between family members.

To everyone who's ever loved someone with fire in their soul and scars on their heart.

To the girls who waited for the right one, and the boys who never thought they were enough.

For those who believe in second chances, slow burns, and wild rides—

And to the "friend" who tried to keep me from finishing this book:

You failed. I finished it anyway.

One

Prologue 20 years ago

Damon

"Tag!" I yelled as I ran by the blonde-haired girl, my friend Jenna, pushing her to the ground as I skidded to a halt, watching her and waiting for the chase to start. The sun was beating down on my back in the field where all the teams parked their trailers at the track, and I felt a drop of sweat start to roll down between my shoulder blades already.

"Ow, Damon," she whined, standing up and smearing dirt from her hands on her highlighter bright pink shirt. I looked at her, taking her in. She looked fine from where I was standing. She probably just wanted me to get close so she could tag me back. I wasn't falling for that one. Again.

"You're fine. Stop being such a crybaby, Gem."

"I am not a crybaby. That hurt me. *You* hurt me." She said, her bottom lip starting to shake and pout.

Her blue eyes turned glassy, threatening with tears. Leave it

1

to a girl to blame me for something I didn't even do. It wasn't as if I was trying to hurt her. I was just playing tag. It wasn't my fault she wasn't moving. I looked her over to make sure she wasn't hurt. My eyes landed on her knee, usually a creamy white now scraped up and covered in blood.

Crap.

I had to come up with something to keep her from tattling and me getting a lecture from our dads, so I distracted her the best way I could.

My mom packed some popsicles, Gem. I grabbed an orange ice pop, and I ripped it open using my teeth. I gave her a popsicle, had her sit down, and got the first-aid kit. She looked at me in confusion as I got out a bunch of the things I'd seen my mom and dad use on me. Dad was always banging or scratching himself on something in here, so I'd seen him do this plenty, and since I was a good helper, I got scratched up too. Didn't even cry about it anymore, but I had a feeling Gem would. I looked at the little wet wipe in my hand, took a deep breath, and said the same thing mom always told me before starting to get me cleaned up.

"This might hurt a bit, Gem."

Those blue eyes got big from behind the popsicle as she stared at me, and I was afraid she was going to start crying or yelling. I had to shut that down real quick.

"It's gonna be ok!" I said quickly, "It'll only hurt for a second, just eat the popsicle and bite down if it hurts too much, ok?"

She nodded, those eyes watching me very carefully, and I felt a funny feeling in my chest as I looked back to her knee, carefully wiping away any dirt or blood. She tensed a bit, but she did good, and then I put the slimy stuff on, and then the band-aid. I thought about kissing it to make it feel better, but that seemed kinda gross. A girl was still a girl, after all.

After she was all bandaged, we were sitting in the back of the trailer, both of us on our fourth ice pop. She slipped off her friendship bracelet she had told me she made the day before. She slid it into my hand, curling my fingers around the pink, blue, and green bracelet in my palm.

"We'll always be friends, Crash." Her soft voice was barely a whisper as she leaned over and pressed a kiss to my lips. The heat in my face dissipated quickly as she pulled away, but the buzz resonated through my body. Maybe kissing and girls weren't so bad.

Two

Jenna

I was picking at the last few bites of my salad, the whines of animals waking up from surgery and other noises of the clinic droning on in the background like white noise. I looked at the clock on my phone and saw that I had a few minutes left on break, and just then, a video call came in from my sister.

She didn't usually call in the middle of the day.

"Hey Sissy, what's up?" I answered, concern edging into my voice.

"Jenna! Oh! You're at work, I'm sorry, but well..." She was practically bouncing all over the screen before holding up her left hand to the camera, "I said yes!"

"Oh, my god! That's amazing!"

"Can you believe it?" My younger sister, Kristen, shrieked in unbridled joy, when her boyfriend- no correction, *fiancé* Mark — came into view.

"I can't believe he proposed." She squealed. I let out a small chuckle, smiling at the two lovebirds.

"I'm so happy for you two!" I chirped, but all too soon I felt an all too familiar ache in my chest.

Truly, I was happy, but I was also the oldest, not that it should have mattered. She found her person in Mark, and I just wanted a taste of what that was like. I'd had friends get married, all of them happy and with their own people, while I was never really able to have that same spark or connection with a man. The alarm on my phone flashed, and I smiled at the happy couple, then feigned a weary groan.

"I have to get back to work; the baby animals won't feed themselves. Congratulations again, you two!" Mark kissed Kristen at the congratulations.

"Sissy, I'll call you as soon as we're back from the trip. Sorry to bother you during your lunch, but you had to be the first to know." She said brightly.

I smiled. "No worries, enjoy the rest of the trip! Mark," I called out as he looked dead at the screen and dipped his chin in acknowledgment.

"Be good to my sister, you hear? You know she's my favorite sister, and I have watched more than enough crime documentaries to make sure you're never found." I teased and then ended the call to the sound of her shouting that she was the only sister.

I stood up and stretched before walking to the baby raccoon enclosure. These furry little bandits had been in my care since they were two days old. Their mother had been injured by a car, and didn't make it through surgery, so these little guys relied on me. I picked up the smallest one of all that I had named Osita. Being the runt, the others would pick on or avoid her, but she kept trying and showed so much spirit for something so small. She was the only one I named because I'd had to work the closest with her, so I felt much closer to her than the rest of her brothers and sisters. We were going to release them soon, and I knew it was going to be difficult to say goodbye to them, but especially her. After I fed them, she tried to play with her siblings but they turned on her real quick, bullying her. I quickly separated her from their gaze and cuddled her until she let out a soft whimpering noise.

As if this day couldn't get any more stressful.

I knew that by the end of the day, I would need a drink or something to take the edge off. So, I quickly sent a text to my best friend.

Me: hey you down to go to the Bullwhip tonight?

Emma: I am sooo down! I need to let off some steam! See you at 7 pm, girly!

Me: I can't wait!

Smiling as I put my phone away; I nuzzled Osita and gave her kisses.

"Tell you what little one, I'll blow off some steam tonight, and get ready for you again on Monday, whatchu think?"

She chirped up at me in reply, and I let her grab at my nose with her tiny paws.

* * *

Finally, the day was over. I pulled up to my house and realized I had just enough time to take a shower and get ready before I had to meet Emma for dinner and drinks; I loved my best friend, but I wanted something more with a guy who was just as crazy about me as I was about him. Stepping out of my scrubs, I sighed as I stepped under the water, allowing the warmth to wash over me. Maybe I would have that spark one day, but there was no use pushing for something that someone else didn't want, not that it seemed like guys wanted anything serious these days, anyway. No need to stress about it. It's not like I had anyone interested in me like that, but who knows if true love actually existed? Lord knows my parents were not the prime example of true love.

They had been married for forty years, and they were *miserable*. They both came to resent each other. Yeah, maybe there was one time they were truly in love and happy, but something must have happened where that was not enough. Especially since dad was a drunk now. Even though Kristen and I reassured them that we'd be fine if they divorced to find happiness again, they both refused. I sighed again, closing my eyes as I washed the shampoo out of my hair and let my thoughts run back to a dark-haired child I vaguely remembered from my past. I pulled myself together and stepped out, checking the time.

I had to hurry up if I was going to make it to The Bullwhip on time. Sliding on a little black dress and loosely curling my hair after I applied a quick bit of makeup, I quickly brushed my teeth before looking in the mirror one last time and applying a bit of highlighter to my high cheekbones and some pink lipstick. I try to smile at myself in the mirror, giving my blonde hair a small shake.

Toss toss.

Finally, I lock up the house and head to the restaurant.

As soon as I am parked, I see Emma in black skinny jeans and a pale pink top waiting near the door. In heels, I jog over to her as quickly as I can and tap her on the shoulder.

"Oh, fuck off! I already told you once, I am waiting for

someone." She huffed through gritted teeth.

"Um, Emma, It's me." I giggled, "I see someone has already hit on you since being here." She spun around, pink spreading across her cheeks.

"Oh my god, Jenna, I am so sorry. You know how the men are in this town. They think "no" means "yes", and get lost means 'I'm yours." She lamented, channeling her inner Megara.

I giggled again and hugged her; "You never have to apologize to me unless you royally fuck up, Ems. Which I highly doubt could happen."

She links her arm with mine and smiles softly; "Let's go in and eat so you can tell me what has been going on with the little bandits and everything that's new!"

When we walk in, we find a seat at the restaurant section and once we've ordered our food; she looks at me like she's looking through me.

"Spill it. Why do you look like someone kicked a puppy?"

I wince at her words. I thought I had done a good job of hiding my feelings.

"I don't know what you're talking about." I rasped.

"Jen, we have been friends for ten years now. I know you like the back of my hand. What's going on? Is it your dad? I know he can be a dick, but don't you dare let him make you miserable just because he's fucking miserable? I know your mama is just as miserable, but she's the one who stays in that situation." She said solemnly, gently closing her hand around mine. I smile softly at this girl that has been by my side through thick and thin.

"Fine, I'll tell you. Kristen and Mark are engaged." I huff, feeling bad that I am not more excited. "Please, don't get me wrong. I am over the moon for my sister and Mark. It's just…"

I trail off, realizing how shitty this is probably coming off.

"You just wish you had someone, too." Emma took a drink from her cocktail, comprehending the situation. I was so surprised I felt my mouth go slightly agape.

The gorgeous brunette across from me let out a laugh and winked at me; "Looks like I hit the nail on the head."

"How do you constantly do that to me?" I huff, letting out a small giggle, relieved at the fact there is nothing I can or have to hide from her.

"Babe, we've been stuck together for ten years. You know me just as well as I know you." She smiles brightly at me before squeezing my hand. "You know there is absolutely nothing wrong with the way you're feeling. If you don't have a date for the wedding, then just like my brother's wedding, when Ricky backed out at the last minute. I'll be your date like you were mine." She laughs.

"Ugh, gross, Ricky! Please tell me you haven't seen that toolbag yet." I implore.

"I know you don't like him, but he's not *that* bad." She crooned as we made our way to the bar and dance area in the back of The Bullwhip after we finished the meal.

"He doesn't love you, Ems. You know that. You deserve better." I complained.

Three

Damon

"Have you seen the news lately?!" shouted Noah, his voice dripping with worry. I popped my head out from under the hood of the car I was working on.

"Clearly fucking not." I huffed. "I've been under the hood all morning. Are you gonna share the news of what's got your panties in a bunch? Or do we need to call a team meeting?" I bit out.

I loved Noah, and he was usually laid back and chill, but when something got up his ass, he made it everyone's problem.

"Well, let's see, 'The Bad boy of drag strikes again.'" He complained, looking from his phone to me, "What is your fuckin' problem?! You said you had a little scuffle at the track. I thought it was just a shoving match, so tell me why videos are circulating of you beating some poor fucker up? What the fuck happened?" he yelled, clearly annoyed as he continued to scroll. "For fuck's sake, Damon, you're the best engine

10

tuner here and one of the best drivers in the state. Why do you continue to compromise everything you and your father built?"

My phone chimed from the workbench, signaling a small truce for now. As I picked it up, I noticed that one of the more recent flings I had programmed her name and number in my phone and sent a risque photo. I rolled my eyes. When were they going to accept that I just wanted them for a night? I wasn't looking for anything serious from these girls because I lived like I raced, and in drag racing, one tiny mistake could send you into the wall.

"Who is that?" Noah asked. He must have seen the annoyance grow on my face.

"Apparently, her name is Nikki." I offered nonchalantly, handing him my phone so he could see the photo. Noah sighed.

"You were with her three days ago and you can't remember her name?"

I laughed. "Sorry, man, she's not anyone worth knowing. She's just a pit bunny." Then another chime came and I let out an audible groan, hoping it wasn't the girl again.

Noah laughed, "Relax, it's just Michael."

Michael was my older brother; he and April, my sister-in-law, had been married about four years and just had my niece late last year. I snatched my phone from him and quickly checked the message. It was a photo of my six-month-old niece Caroline wearing a little onesie that had a light tree on it that read: 'My uncle is faster than yours' I smiled; I swear this little girl was my kryptonite.

"Hey Noah, you and the guys wanna go to The Bullwhip tonight?" I smirked at him.

Noah sighed. "If I'm there, I might be able stop you from

doing something stupid."

I just laughed it off. *"Sure* you will Noah."

*   *   *

When we got to The Bullwhip, I got us a table in the VIP section near the dance floor. We were never too interested in the food situation when we came here, but it was the best spot in town to find some fun and some trouble for the night. That said, I couldn't shake the feeling something big was going to happen tonight. What? I have no idea, I only ever got this feeling before a race. I took a sip of my whiskey, looking over at Noah, eyeing him for a moment. The guy looked so out of his comfort zone.

"Man, relax, you're going to make me anxious if you keep acting like that." I rasped.

Noah took a long drink from his Old Fashioned, "You know this ain't my scene, my guy, it's yours." He chided.

He wasn't wrong. I had been coming here ever since I was eighteen, a year after dad's passing. I coped by drinking and street racing since they wouldn't let me back at the track for the rest of the season after dad passed and even the whole next season. It wasn't fair. I know I spiraled, but I now had a reputation to uphold, "The Bad Boy of Drag Racing." Drag Racing may not have been everything in Lancaster, Montana, but it was a big enough deal that folks would more than likely know me.

Taking another drink of my whiskey, I looked out over the group below when I saw a pretty little blonde slide up to the bar. I swore I felt something in my head say *"home"*.

I shook my head and smirked at Noah, finishing off my

whiskey, "I'm going to get another drink," I winked at him and moved before he could stop me.

"Damn it Damon, get back here!" I heard him shout at my back. Carefully ignoring him, I expertly weaved in and out of the crowd, sliding up to the blonde. She was about a foot shorter than me, but it wasn't hard to be shorter than me since I was six foot two. I drank her in; she seemed so familiar and yet so foreign at the same time. She side-eyed me as she was trying to get the bartender's attention, so I smirked and waved him down.

"What can I get you?" the bartender asked.

"Oh, come on!" she muttered under her breath. I repressed a chuckle.

"A whiskey neat for me and whatever she wants." I looked at her and threw her a wink and a smile. For a very brief moment, I saw her cheeks flush, and I felt my chest swell with pride. Her flushed cheeks and her pretty pink lips wrapped around my cock filled my thoughts.

"I will have two Fairy Juices then, please." She smiled at the bartender, then at me. "Thank you." She exhaled.

Something was clearly upsetting her, and I, for whatever reason, wanted nothing more than to fix it. So, I turned on the charm and I smiled at her.

"You know I have your name tattooed on my ass. And if you are truly thankful, join me back in the VIP area." She gave me a weird look like I was crazy, shit did I misread the situation?

She scoffed, "First off, we just met, so you don't know my name, and second, who do you think you are, Steve-O? Sorry, I can't. I'm here with someone." Of course, she was here with someone. She was gorgeous, too gorgeous to be alone.

"Then he should be the one getting the drinks, not sending

the lady to get them." I growled. Her blue eyes lit up, and her shoulders started shaking as her laughter bubbled up. Why was she laughing, and why was it the most magical thing I had ever heard?

"What is so funny?" I chided. When the bartender returned with our drinks, she was wiping tears from her eyes from laughing so hard.

"I'm s-sorry. You look like you got the wrong impression." She says, still laughing.

"Care to shed some light on the situation?" I pressed. She smiled the sweetest smile.

"I'm here with my best friend and she is getting us a table, though she'd love for us to join you; tonight is a girl's night. Maybe another time?"

Okay, I could handle this. I scratched the back of my neck awkwardly.

Four

Jenna

Watching this hot as hell, tall, fit, tattooed dark-haired man in front of me go from being cocky to embarrassed in a matter of seconds was extremely endearing. I felt an ache rising in my core, something in me yearning for this man beside me. My hand playfully found his muscled chest while I giggled at his predicament.

What the hell, this wasn't like me.

I normally could keep my sexual desires in check. The weird thing is I felt as though we had known each other in a past life or something.

So, I smiled at him and held my hand out, "I'm Jenna Moore, and you are?" he looked a little shocked at me asking who he was.

"I'm Damon West, Jenna Moore? That name sounds... vaguely familiar." He said as he shook my hand. I committed his name to memory.

"This is probably another setup for your cheesy pickup lines. Well, Damon West, if we meet again, your whiskey neat will be on me. I better get back before my best friend sends SWAT for me." I smiled, grabbing my drinks and heading back over to Emma. Knowing he was watching, I put a little extra into my walk.

"Oh my god, Jen, where have you been? I was about to come to find you." Emma barked.

I laughed. "I was at the bar; it's crowded in here, but I have to tell you I met the hottest guy I have ever seen."

"What?! Spill!" She said eagerly.

"He is so tall, has tattoos, fit as hell, has dark hair, and brown eyes. In fact, he bought us these drinks." I snickered.

"Tell me you got the mystery man's name, and if he has any single friends or a brother!" she pressed.

"His name is Damon West, and he said something about being in the VIP area." I looked back at the bar, hoping to see him again, but he was no longer there.

"Hm, that name seems familiar. Oh well, let's go dance!" she said, taking her drink from my hands and taking a long sip. "Thank you, Damon, wherever you are!"

I laugh and follow her out to the dance floor. After dancing for a while, I suddenly felt eyes on me so I looked up in the direction I felt the stare coming from, VIP, and there Damon was watching me, a desire burning in his eyes. I kept dancing, putting on a little show for him. By the next song, he was making his way to me. His hands landed on my hips as soon as he was in front of me and we danced to the music. Before long, his lips were on mine.

Wait! Stop! We don't know him, my brain screamed; this wasn't like me but my god this man could kiss. Before long, he

16

pulled me to a hidden spot between the restaurant and saloon where he picked me up, pressing my back to the icy wall as he kept kissing me.

"Come home with me," he growled, rolling his hips, pressing his growing erection into my sex. Panting, I nodded in agreement. He set me down gently, then pulled me back to the bar entrance. Before we got inside, I gently tugged my hand away. He turned, looking at me with confusion, but the desire made his brown eyes almost black. "Kitten, what's wrong?" he asked tenderly, and my heart flipped in my chest. He tucked a curl behind my ear; "Take a deep breath and talk to me." He instructed.

"I- I've never done this," I muttered, covering my mouth with my hand, embarrassed.

"Wait, wait, wait, you're a virgin?" He questioned as a puzzled look crossed his face.

"Oh God, no, I meant I don't do one-night stands." I blushed at my words.

He smiled at me, and I had to stop myself from melting to the ground.

"Don't worry Kitten, I can't explain it but this is going to be more than a one-night stand." He flashed a wink at me and then pressed a kiss to my lips before leading me back to our table. I grabbed my belongings and hugged Emma and promised I would call her tomorrow. As I felt his eyes traveling up and down my curves, they stopped and lingered on my ass. I turned towards him and smiled, trying to hide my nerves.

"You ready to go, Kitten?" his voice dropped an octave.

Five

Damon

Fuck, she is gorgeous. She gently flitted her fingers on an old friendship bracelet I had hanging on my rear-view mirror, sitting in my passenger seat like it's hers.

No, it is already hers.

What am I thinking? This is *not* me. My head shook to clear my thoughts as my hand slid onto her bare thigh, and I gently squeezed. I was feeling like I was sixteen again. I took a deep breath and exhaled it slowly.

"Do you like speed?" I asked, glancing at her to catch her nervously chewing on her lip. I worried for a moment that I made her decide against everything she was feeling.

Then she looked at me and smiled.

"Yeah, I like a bit of speed. My dad used to take me to the track a lot when I was young…" She trailed off, and in response, I opened the throttle a bit to test the waters. The acceleration pushed us back into our seats, and she let out a gasp. A long moment, and a lot more speed later, I glanced over when she let out a squeal.

"You're crazy, West!" She laughed.

"More than you know, Moore." I conceded with a smirk. After the longest and shortest drive of my life, we pulled up to my house.

This is so unlike me. Why didn't I just take her to a hotel room? I silently questioned myself. I pulled the car into the garage, turning off the engine as I looked at her.

"Are you ready to go in?"

Instead of a verbal answer, her hands framed my face, and she kissed me deeply. I kiss her back, my tongue swiping her bottom lip for access to her mouth, which she granted. As soon as my tongue was in her mouth, my hand dove into her hair as the other sought refuge on her neck, pulling her closer. She moaned and melted into my touch. I move her the best I can in the cramped car, so she is facing me, straddling me, in the driver's seat. My hand caressed her, all the way down her back to her supple ass, and I began kissing her neck. I felt her hips roll against my erection as she moaned again.

Fuck me, if my pants get any tighter, I'm going to bust a seam.

I slid her dress up for better access to her creamy skin, and moved my hands to the front of her, teasing her over the silky, delicate fabric of her panties that she's already beginning to soak through. She gasps, and I chuckle against her neck while I rub the fingers over the damp spot, feeling the outline of her against the fabric and imagining the taste of her on my tongue, the feel of her pussy squeezing my cock.

"What?" She moaned, pressing and rolling her hips down along my pants and against my hand.

"Just admiring how wet I've got you already."

She pulled away and her ass hit the horn, causing it to echo off the garage walls. She jumped under my hands and laughed, the sound so contagious that I had no choice but to laugh along.

"How about we take this inside? I cannot wait to see and feel every bit of you in my bed." I growl softly, nudging her jawline by her ear. She moaned softly in reply, and I couldn't help but nip at her neck.

"C'mon Kitten, let's go so I can hear more noises come out of your sexy little mouth." She catches her breath and nods, so I open the door, allowing her out first. I bite my lip as her ass is directly in my face. I gave her ass a spank, and she let out a surprised squeal.

After exiting the car, she jumped into my arms and wrapped her legs around my waist, one of my hands digging into her ass while she kissed, licked, and sucked my neck gently.

I have *never* entered my house faster.

I pressed her against the back of the door in my effort to get my damned shoes off, kissing any part of her skin that I could reach. I made our way up the stairs, damn near sprinting to my bedroom, set her down, and made sure to keep her in my grasp so that she wouldn't fall. Before she began unbuttoning my shirt, she placed her hands on my chest and looked up at me, her eyes half-lidded with desire. I could feel the desire burning in my chest, and my cock throbbing to be freed. Although I had slept with plenty of women, I knew it would be a memorable night.

Six

Jenna

I unbuttoned his black button-down shirt; he watched me like a wolf tracking its prey. I slowly slid his shirt back to reveal his muscled chest and even more tattoos. Scanning down his body, I noticed something catching in the light on his nipples. I licked my lips automatically.

"See something you like, Kitten?" A chuckle escaped his lips.

"You," I said with a sigh. My hands went to his belt and waistband when he stopped me.

"Nuh-uh, beautiful, I need you out of that dress before I explode." His voice was low with lust, and he bit his lip as he watched me hungrily.

My hands went to the hem of my dress eagerly, but his hands stopped mine in place and he raised his eyebrow at me. I moved my hands out of his way.

He growled, "Good girl," and lowered himself smoothly to his knees, "now, put your hands on my shoulders, Kitten, and allow me" he instructed. When I slid my hands to his shoulders, he lifted my foot gently and unbuckled my shoe, kissing my calf as he did so. I bit my lip and stared down at him, watching him smirk at me and move on to the other leg, repeating the same actions he did with the first.

In a whimper weighted in need, I pleaded, "Damon, baby, please give me more of you." He slowly slipped my dress up to expose more of my legs and nipped at my thighs.

"Patience, kitten," he teased, "We've got all night and I plan to make the most of it."

Once again, I whimpered in anticipation as he pulled my dress up my thighs, exposing my lavender thong. He groaned, pressing his lips to the fabric and kissing the damp spot that he caused. I softly moaned at the touch of his lips against me.

He looked up at me; my eyes instinctively found his, and he flashed that gorgeous grin at me.

"That's right, that's my good girl; those eyes belong to me. Keep them right here."

Oh fuck.

I felt a wave of heat flow to my core in response to his words.

He stood once the dress reached my chest. After he kissed my navel, he slid the dress higher. The fabric briefly covered my eyes as he grazed his teeth across the lacy material covering my nipple. I shuddered as he bit down gently, and then I yelped, which became a moan. I heard his deep chuckle as he kissed my neck again and pulled the dress entirely off, leaving me in nothing but my bra and thong. Before I could protest, he undid his pants and slid them off, along with his socks. I realized he had a lot of tattoos and I wanted nothing more than to lick all the way down his chest and abdomen to his boxers.

"You are so fucking gorgeous," he whispered, his eyes

drinking me in from my head all the way to my legs. I could feel a flush rising as my body reacted to being appraised so openly, but I was doing the same to him.

I slid my fingers down his chest as he kissed me deeply, then fluttered my fingers over his pierced nipples. As we kissed again, he lifted me into his arms with ease, and I felt my bra come undone and the cool air on my breasts for the first time. He gently laid me on the bed; he worked his tongue and lips over my neck and down my body to the top of my thong. He lifted my hips in his powerful hands and I inhaled sharply as the cold air hit my wet pussy.

"Goddamn, you really are so wet for me already Kitten." He chuckled as he leaned down, pressing a kiss to the inside of my thigh before swiping his thick finger through my slit. I moaned out loud.

"God, I can't *fucking* wait to taste you." He groaned. He wrapped his arms around my thighs and pulled me toward him as he slowly ran his tongue over my already sensitive pussy, moaning as he savored me. My hand flew to his hair and gripped as I moaned and squirmed against his mouth. His large hands gripped my hips hard, digging into my flesh. The delicate balance of pain and pleasure felt amazing. His tongue felt incredible on my clit and I quickly felt myself about to crash over the edge.

"Damon, baby, I'm going to come." I whimpered. He moved one hand down so his fingers could work me simultaneously with his tongue.

"Good, come for me, Kitten." His mouth hummed around my clit, and that's all I needed to come undone. I tugged on his hair as I rode out my first orgasm in his mouth. As I came down, I pulled him up to my face and kissed him hungrily, tasting myself on his lips and tongue. He pulled away, and I whined at the loss of his body. He smiled down at me as he stood up and shed his boxers, and his cock sprang forth. My mouth went agape when I noticed not only were his nipples pierced, but so was his thick cock. He opened a condom with his teeth and rolled it onto his length, then hovered on top of me. He kissed me, pulling his lips away, placing his forehead to mine.

"Guide me in, Kitten." He commanded.

Seven

Damon

After our first night together, I woke up with Jenna wrapped up in my arms. I didn't want to wake her, so I kissed her gently on her temple. She smiled as she slept. Then I quietly got out of bed, put on some gray sweatpants, and went down to make us coffee and breakfast. As I was turning a piece of thick French toast, I felt a presence slide up behind me.

"Ooh, that smells fantastic. You cook, you make me orgasm more than once. What can't you do, West?" she asked in a playful tone as her manicured fingernails slid across my tatted chest and I felt her nuzzle into my back. I chuckled and ran my fingers through my hair.

"Good morning, pretty girl, I made us breakfast since we worked off any food we ate yesterday," I said teasingly.

I turned to kiss her forehead, and I realized she was wearing my shirt from last night. Seeing her in that made my cock twitch involuntarily in my pants and she must have felt it since

25

she let out a small giggle. While I continued to fix breakfast, I held her in my arms between myself and the stove. I kissed her cheek, my brain screaming at me,

What are you doing, jackass? This isn't you. With everything you've done, do you really think you deserve something this nice?

I shook my head to clear my thoughts and covered the action by burying my face in her hair and kissed her gently on the nape; she moaned softly in response.

Before talking myself out of it, I pulled out my phone and told her the truth.

"Put your number in. To be honest, Kitten, I rarely take people's phone numbers." I felt her tense up.

"Why me then?" I could barely hear her whisper. Once again, I was honest.

There's something different about you; I don't know why. Although: We haven't known each other long, I can't shake this feeling of familiarity, and I think I'd like to get to know you better.

I set our plates on the table for us to eat, and she took my phone and pressed some numbers and her name into it. As we sat across from each other, she broke the silence first.

"This is delicious, and" her voice trails off, so I reach across to touch her hand gently for reassurance. I fixed my eyes on her and smiled sheepishly.

"I am here to listen to you." I said with assurance.

"You're not the only one feeling... *something*." She said, tearing her eyes away from me. I smiled, then I heard a knock at the door. Confusion led me to excuse myself from the table to answer it. My first reaction upon opening the door was regret, because there stood Nikki.

"Did ya miss me, baby?" she cooed.

My regret quickly changed to irritation. "What the fuck are you doing here?"

"Well, when you didn't answer my text I got worried," she said, feigning concern. I didn't get the chance to answer before Jenna showed up with surprise and hurt etched all over her face.

"Jenna, wait, this isn't what this looks like." I pleaded. She held up her tiny hand, the same one she had digging into my back the night before.

"You don't have to explain anything to me, Damon. I'm going to change and I'll leave." Even though she looked like she was going to cry, she kept her voice in check. Jenna ran upstairs and, true to her word, changed and left my house in under five minutes. In the meantime, I glared at the fucking Pit bunny standing in my doorway.

"Seriously, Nikki, get the fuck out of here!" I said as Jenna squeezed past us, fleeing toward the street.

"Wow, I heard you were a man whore, but I didn't expect you to find a new girl three days after we hooked up." She said sarcastically.

"What the actual fuck is wrong with you? I told you that there would be nothing between us except that one night!" I shouted.

"That's bullshit Damon, you're the best driver at the drag strip. I am the hottest girl at the track. We could have been track royalty."

I scoffed.

"You are hardly my type. You were just something to hit, then quit. The only things that happened were you sucking me off, then I fucked you. Then I fucking left. What the fuck gave you the delusion that we would be together more than

27

that night? I took you to a hotel, so a more important question is, how did you find out where I live?" I screamed, clenching my fists to my side.

"I was at the Bullwhip last night; I saw you with *that girl*. So, I followed you two back here." Her voice dripped with disgust. I moved slightly closer to her, and she flinched.

"Get the fuck out of my house. Don't bother contacting me again and if you do or if I see you near my house, I will call the fucking cops." I growled.

I saw the color drain from her face before she turned around and ran away from the house. After I slammed the door and returned to the dining room to finish cleaning up, I noticed Jenna rinsed off her plate in the sink.

Immediately, I slammed my own plate into the sink with a shout of "GODDAMN IT! "

I knew I wouldn't be able to calm myself down at my house, so I decided to go to the garage and begin working. I ran upstairs, took a quick shower. And as the water ran down over my head I sighed. This felt like punishment. Upon stepping out of the shower, I wrapped my towel around my waist, and looking in the mirror, noticed red marks on my chest and shoulders peeking through the black ink on my skin. After putting on a black T-shirt and jeans, I left home. Once I arrived at my garage, I pulled the '69 Camaro in and started disassembling the car. Although she wasn't much, she was a good backup car. When a bolt wouldn't loosen, I could feel my anger boiling over and I threw a wrench, screaming, "Fuck you, piece of shit!"

I slammed my hands against the frame.

"Damn, man, what did the car do to you?" Noah asked as he handed me a drink.

"I didn't think anyone else was here." I grabbed the drink from him and glared at him, huffing.

"Yeah, well, I have a few projects that need some extra work; the busy season is coming up soon."

"Wow, man, we need to get you laid. Can't be spending all your time here. People will get the wrong idea." I said teasingly.

He scoffed. "Yeah, well, you sleep around enough for the both of us."

Instead of rebutting, I kept my mouth shut, forming a thin line with my lips.

"Wow, something must have really happened because usually at this point you're getting me details to the prior hook up, usually it's something like 'they gave some good sloppy toppy'. What the fuck happened, man?" he asked, clasping his hand on my shoulder.

"I- I think I met someone." I said, still not really believing it.

"Wow, that is not what I expected you to say. I mean, I don't know what I expected, but that was definitely not it." he stammered.

"Yeah, but I am pretty sure I will never see her again." I sighed, defeated

"Well, why the hell not?' He questioned.

I hung my head in shame, "Because fucking Nikki showed up this morning while Jenna and I were having breakfast." I complained, picking up a tool on the workbench and setting it down again.

"Nikki showed up at the hotel you took Jenna to?" he asked for clarification.

"No, I took Jenna home. To my house." I clarified.

"Damn, that sucks, *wait,* you took her to your house?!

Fucking why? Also, how did Nikki know where you live? I thought you took Nikki to a hotel like you usually do with your hookups."

"Damn it, Noah, I don't really wanna talk about it, but fine, here's the story. Nikki and I went to the hotel, but you know me. Normally I get head, then I fuck them and leave, not Jenna. I took her to my house and afterward we slept and I woke up with her in my arms. Then Nikki knocked on the fucking door. Apparently, she was at the Bullwhip last night and saw Jenna and me and followed us to my house and came back this morning. She was calling me baby... it was sick." I explained.

"That fucking sucks dude. I'll tell you one thing though, it sounds like you might not want to let that Jenna chick just walk away without trying." Noah shrugged.

Jenna

I rode in the taxi to my house in a daze, and I couldn't believe what was happening. After I got home, I called Emma. I almost didn't expect an answer, as she was NOT a morning person. To my shock, she answered on the second ring.

"What happened? Where are you? How'd it go?" she said groggily.

"I'm back at home. He has, or may have had, a girlfriend." I whined softly.

"Are you kidding me?! He told me he was *single*! Don't you move, I will be there in ten minutes."

Knowing that was a bit of an exaggeration on her part, I decided to get in the shower and wash the night off of me. I reflected on the past twenty-four hours as I let the hot water cascade over my hair and skin. I felt ashamed. Not about Damon, exactly, though he was part of it, but I felt guilty about not feeling as enthusiastic for my little sister as I should have been. Part of it was jealousy, I knew I was feeling lonely better than anyone, but another part was knowing that now our mother would be even less subtle in her nagging about when it would be my turn. That's what it was, more than anything. My mother meant well, but she sometimes couldn't help giving us a sigh and a wistful look whenever our friends or family members got married, or announced that they were expecting. Every time she did, or made comments about how life was so much easier with a good man, how some outfit would be just perfect for a little grandbaby, I died a little inside.

Then there was Damon himself. I couldn't shake him from my thoughts, no matter how hard I tried. The way his hands felt on me, those soft brown eyes, his hunger, his familiarity. Things felt more right with him than I thought they could, beyond being good in bed. I felt the water start to go cold and realized that no amount of rinsing could get those thoughts washed down the drain.

After my shower, I threw on a tank top and some light cotton shorts, and tossed my hair in a ponytail with a scrunchie, about an hour after I was dressed, the doorbell rang, and there stood my best friend in joggers and a tank top holding two pints of ice cream and two bottles of wine.

"I got us both Triple Chocolate. This feels like a full two pints, two bottles emergency."

She breezed past me to the kitchen to grab two wine glasses and smiled over at me while she opened the wine.

"Make yourself useful and grab us a couple spoons; would you?"

I laughed at her commanding attitude and gave her a salute while moving to get the spoons.

"Aye, aye captain, and is there anything else I can do? You

know I live to serve."

"Smartass, but yes, what're we gonna watch? Need something appropriate to go with the wine..."

We were sitting on my couch, arms linked, heads together, watching our second sappy romance movie, a small pile of tissues growing between us, and empty wine glasses sitting on the table waiting to be refilled. She turned her head to me and kissed the top of my head. "When you are ready to talk about it, we will." She whispered.

Sighing, I paused the movie. "I guess I'd rather do it now than keep dragging it out," I admitted, defeated. She positioned herself facing me, waiting patiently.

"Last night was amazing. Like, *really* amazing. We went back to his house and Ems, I know you noticed his tattoos. He was *covered* in them *and* he had pierced nipples. And God above, can he kiss, made me orgasm more than any guy ever has before, then held me the whole night, and in the morning *made us breakfast*! He said he doesn't take anyone's number, but he took mine. Which, if all that's true, then why did this *bimbo* show up calling him *baby*." Emma made a sympathetic noise and wrapped her arms around me while I nuzzled my head against her shoulder.

"Maybe she was an old fling that just didn't get the hint. I mean, when you went to the bathroom, he told me he was single, but his eyes never left the direction you went," she soothed. "Look, just please give him another chance if he does come back."

I looked at her, puzzled. "Since when have *you* been a romantic?"

She laughed.

32

Eight

Damon

I guess Noah had a point; I grabbed my phone and typed up message after message, but none of them sounded right.

Me: Hey Jenna, it's Damon.

No, that doesn't work.

Me: Hey Kitten, it's Damon.

I sigh. *Why is this so damn hard?* I thought. Finally, I settled on.

Me: It's Damon; I know you probably don't want to hear from me, but I want a chance to explain myself. Please meet me at The Olive Blossom at 7 pm in two days. I promise I'll explain everything.

I sighed again, putting my phone on the workbench, and continued working on the Camaro until I heard a chime. I glanced at my phone. I could hardly believe it, Jenna texted back.

Jenna: Sure.

How the fuck did I get so lucky? For a longer period than I want to admit, I stared at my phone, smiling like a damn fool.

"Well, well, look at that smile!" April, my sister-in-law's voice, came from in front of me. I sat my phone down and looked up, sure enough, there was my entire family standing there. I crossed over and took Caroline from my brother's arms.

"What can I say? I have a date in a couple days." I said, kissing my niece's cheeks.

"A date?" questioned my older brother.

"A date, date?! Ugh, you're getting my princess dirty!" April complained.

"Is there any other date? And she doesn't seem to mind it." I laughed, blowing raspberries on her stomach.

"I, for one, have so many questions. Like, who is this mystery woman that my son deemed so special to take out on a date?" My mama said.

Bouncing the cooing baby in my arms, I looked at my mama, "A woman named Jenna Moore." I stated happily.

"I haven't heard that name in over 10 years!" my mama squealed.

I was so puzzled, but before I could ask any more questions, Michael spoke up. "Well, we were going to invite you out to lunch with us, but we don't want you dirtying up any of the nice places around here."

I cocked my eyebrow.

"Please, any of these places would be lucky to serve someone so refined as my esteemed person." I quipped.

"Wow, used all the scrabble words you know on that one, huh?" Noah chimed in.

"First of all, fuck you-"

"LANGUAGE!"

"Damon! I am SHOCKED at you, I know I raised you better than that!" Mama shot daggers at me.

"I'm sorry, ma'am," I said sheepishly.

"Don't apologize to me, apologize to your niece, then go and wash that filthy face of yours and get ready to eat."

* * *

I told them about meeting Jenna over lunch and concluded with us being interrupted by Nikki.

"So, I take it your first encounter wasn't great?" April asked, teasing Caroline in her high chair. Noah chuckled knowingly.

"Apart from that last moment, it was amazing. I offered to take her out to dinner to explain everything, and get to know her better, and that's where we're at now."

"Tell me you didn't treat her like one of those trashy Pit Bunnies." Mama hissed.

"I can promise you I didn't, ma'am. But why are you so concerned about her? You said you 'hadn't heard that name in over ten years' what does that mean?" I said with caution. I might be ready to fight just about anyone and everything but my mama.

Believe it or not, I didn't have a death wish.

"You really don't remember; her daddy is Donovan. Donovan Moore, he used to race with your dad; they were best friends at the track. She used to come with him and her family and you two used to play when you guys were six. After your father passed away, Donovan fell off the face of the earth. He was the one racing against your dad in that last race." Her voice got quieter with each word.

35

I took her hand and squeezed it, while Michael did the same with her other hand.

"I remember that, and him. God, I can't believe I forgot we were inseparable. I still have the friendship bracelet she gave me hanging from my mirror as a good luck charm."

"So, I think what your mom is saying is that you better be good to this girl or we'll have to fight," Noah warned, nodding at my mama trying to lighten the mood.

I smirked at him, knowing that I owed it to her and myself to make things between us right.

Nine

Jenna

I came out of the bathroom and nearly walked into Emma practically bouncing outside the door.

"You have a date, Jen-Jen." She cooed.

I stared at her, bewildered. "With you?" I asked, raising my eyebrow.

"No silly, Damon, at the Olive Branch. You are meeting him at 7 in a couple days. I really do think you guys should talk, hopefully this was all a stupid misunderstanding."

I rolled my eyes.

"Ugh, fine, I'll hear him out," I huffed. There was no use fighting her. When Emma set her mind to something, that was it.

"Good girl," she said sweetly, "come on, let's get your outfit picked out so you don't have to worry about it the day of.

I reluctantly let her drag me to my room. Almost immediately, dresses, skirts and occasional lingerie came flying out of my closet and onto my bed.

"Emma, stop! I am going to have to clean this up alone!" I laughed. After a few seconds, she pulled out a short red dress with a sweetheart neckline and held it up to me.

"This is perfect. Pair it with your black heels that have the bow on the back. Wear your hair down, beach curls, and finally… glam makeup." She advised me.

"Oh? Are you gonna do my hair for me too?" I questioned teasingly.

"Obviously. I am going to make you so hot he'll be questioning whether you're even in his league." She said so matter of factly I could only roll my eyes in reply.

"Wait, why am I meeting *him* there, shouldn't he be picking me up?" I asked.

"Give me your phone, you're right. I am remedying this egregious oversight." She smirked.

"No, no, it's okay, really, I was just curious." I stammered. Emma then jumped at me, tackling me onto my bed, and my clothes.

"Give me the phone, Jenna! Know your worth, and after this morning, you're right, he needs to go the *full* distance. Phone. *Now.* Don't make me find it on my own." she said, staring into my eyes while she was crushing me. I squealed as she started to tickle me.

"Fine, fine, geez, Ems you're not fair," I said, wheezing, handing over my phone.

"Change of plans Damon, you can pick me up from my house at 645. Sharp. And sent! Right now all we need to do is get your hair done on the day…" she said devilishly.

Approximately two days, four panic attacks, and an hour later, Damon was outside my door in a form-fitting navy blue button-down and dark-washed jeans with a box of chocolates in one hand, and a bouquet of sunflowers and white rose in his other. Emma stood behind me beaming like a proud parent.

"You just gonna stand there looking dumb or are you gonna say something, slick?" she asked, her voice dripping with sarcasm.

"Wow, you look… breathtaking," he whispered, and for a moment I swear I saw him blush.

"Looks like my job here is finished," Emma announced, "be good to her, West, or I *will* hunt you down." She said teasingly as she squeezed in between us on the way to her car.

"I will. Oh, uh, J-Jenna, these are for you." he stammered, handing the flowers and chocolates to me.

With a smile I breathed in the aroma of the flowers, "Let me get these into some water, then we can leave." He cleared his throat. It kinda made me happy to know he was a little nervous.

Good, asshole. You're lucky I am even going to hear you out after the other morning.

I shook my head to clear the negative thoughts. After placing the flowers in a vase with water, I walked back to the front door to see Damon staring at an old photograph that was taken when I was about six years old. It was our racing family that was no longer together, my dad and his friend were in the center with mom and his wife beside their respective husbands, me and a dark-haired boy were together, it was a candid shot where we were all laughing. The look in Damon's eye was so emotional, but something said not to ask about it right now. I snipped the base of the flowers and arranged them before heading back to my tall, dark, and handsome date.

"Alright, the flowers are in the vase and I am ready whenever you are." I smiled while whispering. He turned to me, giving me a dazzling smile.

"Let's go, Kitten." He said, offering me his hand. I took it before I could decide against it. Once we were in the car, the silence was deafening. I glanced at him, shifting gears in the driver's seat. I chewed on my lip nervously.

"Stop that kitten, you're going to hurt yourself," he warned softly.

Ten

Damon

I haven't spoken a word since we left her house. That picture she had hung up caught me off guard. It confirmed what my mom said, not that she had a reason to lie to me. I just wasn't expecting it. Why couldn't I remember this gorgeous girl beside me? I finally spoke up when I noticed her chewing on her lip.

"Stop that kitten. You're going to hurt yourself." I warned softly.

This is the second time I've seen her doing that. It's a dead giveaway that she is nervous and overthinking. At the sound of my voice, she stopped and her mouth popped open in surprise.

"How did you know?" she asked.

"Just because I'm watching the road doesn't mean I can't see you out of my peripheral." I chuckled, pulling up to the restaurant.

She got ready to open her door, "What are you doing?" I

questioned.

"I was going to get out of the car?" She looked at me, confused.

"No, just wait until I open your door. Please?" I smiled at her, and she fidgeted in her seat.

"Okay." she whispered.

She must have had shitty boyfriends. I can't believe Donovan let that happen.

Oh, so now you think you are boyfriend material.

I shook my head to clear my intrusive thoughts and smiled down at her as I opened her door. I offered her my hand to help her out. She hesitated before reaching out her hand to mine. I'm not going to lie, that stung. Once we got inside, I gave them my name and they led us to a secluded table. Before she could sit, I pulled her chair out for her.

"Such a gentleman." She teased.

"What can I say, my mama raised me right." I chuckled, crossing to my side of the table. I ordered a bottle of their sweet red wine before I started talking.

"Jenna, I need to explain some things," I began as she sat down her menu, gently looking at me, and waiting for me to continue. My collar now seemed too small for my neck.

"I know the reputation I have with women, and it's true; I honestly have been a bit of a man whore. That's why I never took girls' numbers before yours. I never wanted anything serious from anyone. I'm not sure why, but meeting you is making me want to give that a shot." I said, maintaining eye contact.

It felt gross acknowledging my past with women that way. She nodded, letting me know that she understood, but her eyes let me know she also had questions, so I waited a moment to see if she'd ask them. She didn't, so I continued, "That woman who showed up the other morning was a fling. There is nothing between us. Honestly, she shouldn't have even known where I lived. She saw you and me at the Bullwhip and followed us to my house. She left, then came back that morning, and well, did what she did. I am so sorry, Jenna."

I took a deep breath waiting for her to respond.

"Wow, that was a lot of information, Damon. I mean, I'll forgive you but I want us to go slow and get to know each other. I *am* still interested in getting to know you, but I'm worried that the playboy is still around. " She responded. I exhaled sharply.

"I can't even begin to tell you how much I want that!" I said, maybe a little too excited. "And I promise, as long as I'm with you, there's no man whorish nonsense."

She just laughed and it was magical.

"So, what do you do for work? Tell me about your family." I asked excitedly.

Again she giggled, "I am a wildlife rehabilitator, I have a younger sister, Kristen, she just got engaged. My dad and mom are a mess. But they're my parents. What about you?" she asked genuinely curious.

"I am a drag racer and owner of Drag Torque, the performance garage. I have an older brother, Michael, he's married to April and they have my six-month-old niece, Caroline. My dad passed when I was eighteen, in a drag race. Mom is still around but she misses him terribly." I said softly.

"I'm so sorry." she lamented squeezing my hand. I picked her hand up and kissed her knuckles.

"It's okay beautiful, he went out doing what he loved," I assured her. "Kitten, I have to ask about the photo you have

43

hanging up in your house, the one with the group of people, do you know who they are?"

"Um, well those were friends of my parents when my dad raced, it's been almost ten years now. I don't actually remember. I hung it up because it's one of the last photos I have that my dad actually is happy in. Everything since then, he's been so miserable. It's like something happened but he never told Kristen or I, and now he and my mother are miserable together at best," she shrugged trying to brush the conversation off.

"I'm sorry Jenna. I didn't know. But the reason I ask is that picture has my dad, my mom, and I in it. Apparently, we knew each other when we were younger. " I stated, watching her face as the shock spread across it.

Eleven

Jenna

"The dark-haired boy was you?! You- you grew up!" I stammered, not hiding my shock.

Damon let out a low chuckle. "In more ways than one. Is it so hard to believe that scrawny little boy was me?" He asked mischievously.

I blushed at his insinuation. "Damon, be good, we're in public," I warned.

"Awe, what happened to the baby? I like when you call me baby. And being in public didn't stop you from making out with me last night." He teased me.

Shortly after, the server brought out our food. For the rest of dinner, we just talked about family and life and got to know each other and after three glasses of sweet red wine, I started talking more about Osita, and the rest of the animals.

"You would love Osita, or you might love the rest of her gaze. They are rambunctious, but she is the smallest and gets bullied a lot." I stopped and sighed, remembering what was to come. "We have to release them soon."

My voice shook with emotion.

"I am gonna be a freaking mess. They have been in my care since they were two days old." I rambled, pouting, and feeling a little tipsy.

I normally don't drink wine. This was an unfamiliar experience. The warmth from the drink started spreading to my face along my cheeks.

"Kitten, maybe you should slow down on the wine. I see the way your cheeks are flushed, and I just keep rethinking about our night together. How flushed your cheeks got, your soft pants, and whimpers," he stated, gently placing his hands on the table.

Watching him, I hungrily looked at his hands and absent-mindedly licked my lips.

"Careful, Kitten. You told me you want to go slow, which is fine with me, but with the way you're going and you looking at me like that..." His glance turned dark. "I'll want to pull you closer and finger you under the table until you come all over my fingers." He growled in a hushed voice as he watched me closely.

Suddenly, I was parched, so I locked eyes with the danger-ously sexy man, who could easily tear my heart out and destroy it beyond repair with such ease, and finished the glass of wine in front of me.

He let out an audible growl.

I smiled at him, maintaining eye contact with him, he used his leg to move my seat to the side, then he pulled the rest of the way until I was seated directly beside him. His full lips were inches away from mine, his lips glossy from him, licking them. He leaned in and kissed me then growled in my ear, "Can you be a good girl, and keep quiet? I wanna feel your soft wet pussy on my fingers."

I whimpered softly, nodding.

"Good Kitten." He whispered as his hand slid under my dress, his fingers brushed against the fabric of my panties. I bit my lip to stop any noise from escaping.

The waiter came up to our table.

Oh. My. Fucking. God.

"Would we like dessert?" He asked politely. Damon looked at me and then the waiter

"Sure, whatever you suggest will be perfect." He said calmly, not moving his hand away from my pussy.

"Okay sir, I will have a surprise right out for you two." The server said unenthusiastically as he turned and left.

He skillfully slid my panties to the side and called for the server to come back as he slipped his middle finger inside me right as the server popped back into view. I fought against the moan that wanted to escape me as he slowly fingered me under the table.

"I know I said whatever *you* wanted, but I decided on a tiramisu and a Caffè corretto, thanks." He said to the server nonchalantly as his finger pulsed in and out of me and his thumb rolled against my clit.

Once we were alone again, he leaned over, kissed me just under my ear and growled, "Good girl, Kitten. You're so worked up for me. I can feel your pussy milking my finger, but I really want you to come on my hand, beautiful."

I whimpered softly, my breath becoming ragged as I fought to keep any composure at all in the restaurant.

Twelve

Damon

The feeling of her gripping my arm, watching her struggle to keep quiet in public, made me so fucking hard I could hardly stand it. At the end of the day, I wanted to do whatever it was that she wanted. Taking it slow was completely fine by me, really.

But now.

Right now, *right* this second, the only thing I wanted to do was get her to come all over my fingers in this restaurant. So I kept rubbing her clit, kept stroking her G-spot, while she did her damnedest to hold her moans behind those pretty lips. The server brought out our tiramisu and the caffè corretto with a smile.

"If you need anything else, sir, please just let me know." He muttered and walked away. I nodded at him and then smiled at her.

"Kitten, can you feed me, please? My hand is…well, a little

busy and you just *feel* so fucking good with how your tight little pussy grips my fingers." I growled in her ear. Jenna's eyes had been half closed, and her fingers dug even harder into my forearm as she fought for her life trying to hide her arousal from the other tables. Her mouth fell open, and her cheeks flushed crimson like they did the previous night. I could feel her growing ever wetter by the moment, and her hands were shaking as she reached for the small dessert fork. Considering that I never once let up with teasing her clit, or g-spot, or both, she was doing remarkably well. The fork was then used to pick up a piece of tiramisu, very carefully steadied with a deep, shuddering breath, then brought and held gingerly against my lips. I licked my lips and took a bite from the fork, savoring the chocolate, the espresso, and the sweet cream. My throat filled with a growl of delight and I licked my lips again before looking at her with a grin.

"Oh, that was *delicious,* kitten, thank you. In fact, I think there is only one way to make this even better."

I held her eyes while I pulled myself from her dripping pussy. I slowly withdrew my fingers from her warm, wet sex, and she whimpered in protest at the loss of them. Smirking at her, I licked one of my fingers clean. Her eyes never left my lips, and I noticed that her hips rolled in the seat as she sought the friction she desperately wanted and whined at me in need. Her eyes were darkened with lust and her breathing was getting heavier as she watched me savoring her delicious little cunt.

"Mmmm… that is so fucking good, Kitten. You just have to taste this for yourself," I said just loud enough for her to hear, holding my fingers and the fork with the rest of the tiramisu to her lips.

Her eyes widened, as if she was surprised at her own actions,

49

and her willingness to do them. Her apparent surprise at those actions did not stop her as she slid her tongue out from those perfect lips and swirled it around my fingers, cleaning all of her off of them before taking the bite of tiramisu. I set the fork back on the plate as she savored the taste, my eyes never leaving her. She moaned out loud as she swallowed the little treat. I leaned over and kissed her ear, trailing down to her neck.

"That's my good fucking girl... but hush now, Kitten, we don't want people *knowing* what I am doing to you in public. How I've got you tasting your delicious little pussy with our dessert, now do we?" I rasped.

Jenna

How did we get here?

How was I licking my arousal off this man's fingers? In public?

What the hell has gotten into me? I mean, I know I am a lightweight but come on! I couldn't be tipsy off two, maybe three glasses of wine.

Could I?

Maybe it was the man beside me. Something about his quiet dominance making me toss all of my inhibitions to the wind. I felt my pussy clench and came just as soon as I put the piece of tiramisu in my mouth. The wine, the filthiness of what we were doing, and the combination with the rich coffee and mascarpone flavors blending in with the sweet wetness of mine, mixed with the saltiness of his fingers, had been far more than enough to send me over the edge.

"That's my good fucking girl," His deep voice dripped with

lust like honey in my ear. I whimpered in response, clenching my thighs and trying to find just some of the friction I needed to keep feeling.

"Are you ready for me to take you home, beautiful?" he whispered against my neck, his breath covering me in goosebumps all over.

I nodded, my eyes half closed and nearly delirious with lust. Fuck, I was hoping for a repeat of the previous night. Him panting, his grunts, and him repeating my name over and over like it was a sacred prayer drove me absolutely fucking wild. I needed him inside me after all this.

Once he paid the check, giving the server what I assume was a very generous tip by the way the server was acting, Damon escorted me gently to his car with his hand gingerly against the small of my back. It never left me as he opened first the door of the restaurant and finally the car door. Once we were safely hidden from the prying eyes of the public in his car, I leaned over and kissed him deeply.

It must have surprised him, my boldness startled me as well. Again, this wasn't normally how I would be on a first, second, or fifty-third date, but I was enjoying his tongue dancing with mine. He was an amazing kisser, firm yet gentle, sensuous and giving. There was no fight for dominance, though if he wanted, he could easily overpower me. He gave me pleasure, now I wanted to reciprocate and my hand went to his belt, but he stopped me. I looked up at him, my eyes imploring but he shook his head slowly.

"Damon, why?" I breathed. There was no way he thought I didn't want this too.

"Kitten, I know you want to go slow, and so I am stopping it right here. I *loved* getting you off, but I don't want you to think *that* is the only reason I am with you. It's not about sex. Though don't get me wrong, the sex is phenomenal. I just want to get to your heart and not *only* your pussy." He gave me a sincere smile that could melt the iceberg that sank the Titanic.

Shivering, I let out a whiny "Fine" and pouted. He rewards me with a laugh and another of those infuriating smiles.

"I promise, Jenna, next time we'll do whatever you want. Right now though, I just want us to go at a pace that *you're* comfortable with." He said with a wink.

All too soon, we're at my house making out in front of the door like a pair of horny teenagers. Only without the threat of parents turning on the light or interrupting.

"Goodnight, Kitten." He says inches away from my mouth before turning from me and walking back to his car.

"Goodnight, tease!" I say to his retreating back and listen to his chuckle as he slips into the driver's seat.

Thirteen

Damon

The smell of gasoline, the cheering of the crowd.

"West! Hey Miles you have 30 mins before you're up for the last pass." Someone yelled.

"I'll be there. Alison, get your sweet ass over to the trailer. I need my good luck charm." My dad shot a wink at my mom.

"Oh, Miles, you're terrible! Not in front of Damon... I will see you there." she giggled as she stood up, pressing a kiss to my forehead. I grimaced.

"He'll understand one day. Guys, we've done well this weekend. Spend time with your families. I know they're around. Damon, why not go see if Don brought his girl you used to like so much," my dad said, ruffling my hair as he passed by. I rolled my eyes, but I got up and started walking around. In a flash, we were rolling up to the staging area. Dad gave mom a kiss and hugged me.

"I'll see you both at the end."

He winked at us, smiling as he climbed into his all-black 1971

Chevelle SS. Mom and I made it to the end and waited for him. He and Donovan pulled up setting off the beams.

I watched, my breath bated, as the tree clicked down. Immediately dad had a holeshot. He went down the torque pulling him into a wheelie, he slammed down on his front wheels, hard. Two seconds later, the horrific sound of screeching tires and dad's car slamming into the right wall and then veering to the left wall. I was holding my mom back from running onto the track. Her tears soaking into my shirt and her screaming his name repeatedly rang in my ears, I just stood there clinging to her as if that would make everything alright.

Forty-eight hours after the crash, he coded.

I woke up in a cold sweat. Only one thought crossed my mind. *I was going to look at dad's car and figure out why his car pulled to the right on that last pass.* Once I got to the garage I sent a text to Jenna.

Me: Morning gorgeous, I hope you slept well, and I hope you have a great day. I'll call you this evening.

I backed the trailer into the garage, and slowly released the wench, lowering the car to the floor.

"Morning, Damon. Why are you looking at your dad's car? We all know the ball joint broke that day which caused him to wreck." Noah asked softly. He was right. I have looked over this car so many times, especially after we got it back from them investigating.

"I know. I have been over it a million times, I just can't shake the feeling that it didn't break on its own. If it did there would have been telltale signs that it was going out, you and I both know that, and there was nothing. Maybe I didn't look as hard as I should have."

I shook my head as I kneeled down slowly taking off the

tires one by one.

Noah's hand clasped my shoulder. "Okay man, give me a second to clock in and I'll help you."

I was looking back at the ball joint when something urged me to look at the other side. I stood up and walked to the front passenger tire.I started looking over the ball joints because if one was wearing out then certainly this one should also be worn out but this side looked brand new.

"Hey, Noah, what are the chances that a brand new ball joint would break immediately?" Anger seethed through my gritted teeth.

"I suppose it could happen, but it is highly unlikely. Why? I take it that side looks brand new?" Noah pondered.

"They were basically brand new, the factory markings are barely scratched," I clicked my tongue in annoyance.

In anger, I turned and left, slamming the door of my office and shoving things off of my desk as Noah yelled for me to return. How hadn't I noticed that they were practically new joints before? A new one usually didn't break after ten turns, something was clearly up. I called in one of our oldest mechanics, one of the guys that had worked with my dad since the beginning, George. Sure he was a grumpy old bastard but he had a heart of gold.

"Hey, George," I greeted the old man who sauntered in my office with a preemptive huff, his facial expression reading 'Fuck off if you know what's good for you.'

"Hey Damon, what can I do ya for?" He greeted back gruffly, taking a slow seat.

"Well, I was taking another look at dad's car," I began.

"Hooey, we known what happened to your dad since the day he wrecked. Why can't ya just let the dead lie?! Someone didn't do their job checking the ball joints," He grumpily stated.

"I know George, I know, but I have never been able to shake the feeling that something was off. I was right, George. Those ball joints were brand new. The factory marks on have a few scratches, and almost no other signs of wear." pausing I take a deep breath and run my fingers through my hair.

I continued "That means that yeah it could have been a faulty ball joint but that's not that likely. What do you think George? Was there anyone that wanted my dad dead?"

He may not have the answers but this guy was like a second father to me, I knew he'd never steer me wrong.

"Well," he pondered "No one was around the car for at least twenty minutes. No one on our team would have hurt your dad. I can tell you that honestly."

Fourteen

Jenna

Going through my tasks for the day after receiving the text from Damon, I thought nothing could bring my mood down. When I made it to the raccoon enclosure I found Osita on the floor bleeding with patches of missing fur. I called for the doctor, who rushed in.

"Let's try to stop her bleeding, then let's get her to the x-ray machine so we can see the damage we're working with. We won't be putting her back with her siblings. That is for sure," huffing he scolded the other raccoons. I wrap her up and take her out and into an old break room that is no longer in use. I apply light pressure to her wounds hoping not to hurt her just to stop the bleeding, her little voice is so weak. We alternated our schedules so there were people here at night and some during the day. Whoever was on duty last night didn't do that job. I held her close crying in pain for her and in anger because someone just let her sibling almost kill her. It was just not fair.

Once the bleeding started clotting I carried her to the x-ray room, talking to her softly explaining what I was doing.

She was too weak to move so she just let me do what I needed to do, when the doctor came in "How's our patient?"

"She has a fractured jaw, but nothing else seems to be broken thankfully," handing him the X Rays photographs.

"Dr. Jackson, I hate to be this person but someone clearly wasn't checking on them last night. When we peek our heads every couple of hours, yes her siblings pick on her and are mean, but they wouldn't have been able to hurt her to this extent and how did no one notice she was on the floor bleeding until I came in?" Anger bubbled up from my throat threatening to turn into tears, I hate that I am an angry crier. The doctor nodded at me "I completely understand and agree, I promise Jenna, we will find out who didn't do their job. They will no longer have a job," shuffling the X-Rays looking at each one he stated softly. "First we need to prepare her for surgery. We need to stabilize her jaw. So since she's stable I am going to let you two take a break before we start her surgery." Deciding to go ahead to introduce Osita to Damon I decided to video chat him after two rings

"Hey Kitten," his voice was more gruff than normal. Something clearly had happened at work. "Did I call at a bad time?" I whispered meekly, sniffling. "No, absolutely not. Why are you crying, Kitten?" concerned he asked I heard the jingle of his keys. So I angle the camera to the hurt baby raccoon in my arms. "Thi-this is Osita. I wanted you to meet her." my voice cracked as I felt the tears leave my eyes. "Hello Osita, you're quite the cute little girl. Jenna will make sure you are completely taken care of I promise." softly he reassured the kit and me. I reangle the camera up pulling myself together.

"Someone didn't do their job last night by checking on the gaze and since she is the runt her siblings tried to kill her. We're about to go into surgery to stabilize her jaw. I wanted you to meet her first." I sighed. "Thank you, Kitten, it means so much to me that I got to meet her. I know how much she means to you." his deep voice was almost a purr. I smiled at him. "I will call you at lunch to let you know how the surgery went." he smiled back before responding "I will be waiting, oh Kitten text me first as I have a meeting with the track, but I don't want to miss any updates on the two cutest girls in the world."

With that reassurance, we hung up and I prepped the tiny raccoon for surgery.

Fifteen

Damon

I pulled up to the track and slowly got out of my car, Noah trailing behind me. "Are you sure we should have left Liam in charge?" he questioned sincerely. I rolled my eyes before replying.

"I have our tuner, the engine builder, and our best mechanic with me. I had to leave someone in charge," I bit out.

"It's been at least ten years Damon, they didn't have cameras in the pit area until the last couple of years. Boy, I don't know what you think you're going to find. I had work to do," gruffed George. I shrugged, annoyed,

"You know you two didn't have to tag along."

"Bullshit Damon! One of my closest friends died and now you're telling me it might not have been a freak accident. Of course I am coming with you. Plus, someone has to make sure you don't do something stupid," George lectured.

Noah nodded. "You're my best friend. Do ya think I would

let you do something stupid to where you couldn't race or keep the garage? You know me better than that."

I checked my phone to see if Jenna had texted me yet, and I smiled at them.

Nothing yet.

I hated not being able to help her or Osita, but we were both having our own rough days and I knew we could talk about them later and get through them together. Her tears over the tiny raccoon just showed how kind she was. That she trusted me was gratifying for me; I knew I didn't deserve it, but I needed to fight to keep it.

Once inside, the president of the racing league met me at the door.

"Damon, what a pleasant surprise, what are you doing here?" He asked.

"How long have you guys had cameras in the pit area, Greg?" I wasted no time.

"About nine years or so. Why?" He pressed.

"So there was none around the time that my father passed," I asked, clenching my fists.

"No, I'm sorry Damon, we put them in after your father's death, he took a deep breath almost as if he was choosing his next words carefully.

"However, we've had some photos show up of that day," Greg said reluctantly. I relaxed my fist as it started to shake, I knew I couldn't do anything without severe consequences. I felt Noah's hand on my shoulder.

"Were you not gonna tell anyone about it, Greggory? What the hell is wrong with you, son? The family deserves to know, well at least *he* deserves to know. He can then discuss it with his brother, and they can decide if Alison needs to know. That womans been through hell and back," George complained.

"Goddammit Greg, what if it had been your father? Wouldn't *you* want to know *any* developments?" Noah snapped.

Greg took a step back.

"The pictures are just like someone was monitoring your pit, before you all walked away, then there is like time missing and you're all back again," Greg winced, realizing the full weight of those implications. A growl emanated from low in my chest, my vision clouding.

"So do you think someone was running surveillance on our area?"

Greg took another step backward.

"Maybe we shouldn't be talking about this in the lobby. Let's go to the conference room." He said hesitantly.

We filed into the conference room, standing around it while he took his seat at the long table.

"So I wanted to examine the photos a bit more before I gave them to you and before I ruffled feathers, your whole family has been through so much already. I didn't want to cause any extra pain if it was nothing." Greg said sheepishly.

"Well, that's bullshit and ya know it." Noah's accent came out more when he was angry. I felt my phone buzz. I was sure it was Jenna sending an update on Osita, I would message her as soon as we finished here. Provided I was in the right state of mind.

"Greg, did you know that his ball joints were basically brand new?" my voice echoed in the small space. I made a show of cracking my knuckles, and I watched Greg's eyes widen and the fleeting look of surprise that covered his face. If you weren't looking at him you would never have known.

"I-I-I didn't," he stammered.

"Do ya know what that means?" Noah asked.

"I -I don't," Greg tried to regain his control.

"You always were the yuppy kind. Never wanting to actually get your hands dirty. It means that unless they were actually faulty then one wouldn't have broken. Do you know how long it takes, Greg, to mess with a ball joint so it 'breaks'?" George stepped in.

"No, I don't," Greg responded, straightening up.

"Well to sabotage one takes less than 5 minutes," George stated matter of factly.

The tension in the air was so thick you could cut into it with a knife. I looked down at the table, then back up at Greg.

"Where did the photos come from Greg?" I asked, crossing my arms so I didn't hit him or do something to ruin me racing this season or worse, sent to jail.

"I- I'm telling the truth I don't know who sent them." he stammered again.

"Bullshit!" Noah jolted up out of his seat. George looked over at him, silently shooting him a fatherly warning like he had been doing to both of us since my dad had passed, and Noah's dad was back in Georgia. Noah sat back down.

George stood up slowly, "Even if you don't know the exact person who sent them you know where they came from, I can see it all over your face. Why are you trying to protect someone who murdered another person? Even if they weren't actually trying to hurt or kill them they still did. Now, Greg,where did the photos come from?" Each step George took towards Greg accentuated his words like a threat.

Sixteen

Jenna

A tense and long hour later, Osita's surgery was a success. I stroked her little paw and her head, waiting on her to wake up and watching her ribs rise and fall with every inhale and exhale.

The vet poked his head in on us, "How is little Osita doing?"

I looked up at him "Her breathing is level and her heart rate is still steady. She should be waking up soon."

He nodded and moved on to the next animal that required his attention. A few moments later Osita was coughing on the ET tube that was in her throat. I stroked her as I gently removed it, cooing at her, "Hello there pretty girl, welcome back! I know you're soo sleepy so you get to stay in this comfy cage for now. I got you a couple of warm blankets, some hot water bottles and a few stuffies to cuddle with. I will be back in fifteen minutes to check on you."

I went to grab a drink from the break room fridge. I pulled

out my phone and sent a text to Damon.

Me: Osita is out of surgery and has opened her eyes. She pulled through!

I waited a couple of minutes and there was no response, so I slid my phone back into my pocket, washed my hands and went back to Osita who was now sleeping peacefully. I checked her heart rate and the rate of her fluid intake, grabbed a thermometer, dipped it into the lube and took her temperature. After I charted her vitals, I went to find the vet. As I was searching for the Doc, I came close to a hallway and overheard voices.

"I can't believe you haven't gotten caught yet," one voice said.

"Sh, keep your voice down. No one but you knows that I have been sneaking around with the doctor," the second voice scolded.

"You're going to be caught soon, especially since Jenna and Dr. Jackson are looking for the person who was on duty in the raccoon enclosure last night, and it was you and Archer!" the first voice stated.

"Don't worry Dr. Thomas won't let them find out, because if they find out it was me then it would expose the affair I am having with him. Even though he keeps telling me he'll leave Amara for me," the second voice scoffed.

I silently took my phone out and snapped a picture of the two of them talking. A few moments later, I walked down the hallway with a smile plastered to my face.

"Oh hello Susan and Carly, have either of you seen *Dr. Thomas* or Dr. Jackson?" I asked. Carly's poker face didn't falter, but a hint of shock crossed Susan's face briefly.

"Oh, hey Jenna. I'm sorry, I didn't see you there. I haven't seen either of them," Carly stated.

"Oh, that's okay, thanks anyway," I said as I started down the hall, "Oh, by the way, I would watch what you talk about in the hallways, you never know who will overhear you," I said over my shoulder. I should have tried to record the conversation but I didn't think there was much evidence there.

There had to be another way to expose her. Lost in thought I collided with something firm.

"Whoa there, Jenna are you okay?" the man's voice pulled me from my thoughts. I looked up into Dr. Jackson's green eyes.

"I'm sorry, Dr. Jackson. I was coming to find you, Osita is resting. I removed the ET tube, um, can we go to your office for a moment?" He needed to know who was slacking off so maybe we could figure out a way to bring it to light.

Once the door closed I tried to spill the information to Dr. Jackson.

"Dr. Jackson," I began, but he cut me off.

"Call me Daniel."

"Uh sure, Daniel... Anyway I found the person who has been slacking off but there is a problem. She's sleeping with Dr. Thomas." He moved slightly closer to me.

"Is this really what you wanted to talk to me about?" He looked me up and down, hungrily.

"Yes? What else would I want to talk to you about, Dr. Jac-Daniel?" I asked as I took a step back.

"I've overheard you venting to Osita many times about wanting someone in your life. Well, Jenna, I am right here," he said matter of factly.

"There are a couple of things wrong with that." I said, holding my hand up for emphasis, "one, and it's huge, you're my boss. Two, I am seeing someone. And three *our* job is to make sure the animals are taken care of and are able to be released. Not murdered by their own kind on our watch. I like you as my boss, but nothing more. Sorry, Dr. Jackson."

He backed away slowly "Oh, I see. Well, I will get you to come around to thinking we could be good together."

I sighed, "No, I am sorry Dr. Jackson, really, I'm flattered, but we work together. Please, listen to me. Carly is having an affair with Dr. Thomas *and* they are sleeping together at work when they were supposed to be doing other things like checking on the patients."

He pinched the bridge of his nose "I know. I *have* told him to stop, at least during the time they're supposed to be working. But, he obviously didn't listen, and now there has to be an investigation."

My mouth popped open in shock and I looked up at him bewildered, "You *knew* she was the reason Osita almost died and you acted like you had no idea how it could have happened! Are you kidding me?!" I shot up like a bullet from a gun, practically running out of his office. I just wanted to get back to my girl, she needed me, and clearly no one else in this place cared about her. That was when I decided to quit and kidnap Osita. So I shot Damon and Emma the same text.

Me: So I think I'm gonna quit, and kidnap Osita. What do you think?

Damon didn't respond. But almost immediately, Emma did.

Emma: Okay, sounds like a half baked plan, why not finish today and call me tonight so we can properly discuss it.

Of course she was right. I needed a better plan, not just quitting and stealing this baby raccoon.

Seventeen

Damon

"It came from Shear Performance," Greg said, shaking slightly, and backing away from George, stopped abruptly when his back bumped the crisp white wall behind him.

"See, was that so hard?" George said, smiling at the clearly terrified Greg.

"I need a fucking cigarette," I muttered under my breath.

Once out of the conference room, I headed to my car to look for my pack of cigarettes that hadn't been touched in a year. I opened the glove box I used to keep them in only to find it empty.

"Lookin' for these, bud?" Noah asked, pulling the cigarettes out of his pocket.

"Yes," I grab them out of his hand and take one out, tapping it on the back of the zippo he handed to me before placing it between my lips, lighting it and letting the smoke fill my lungs and calm my nerves, running my hand through my hair.

"Fuck," the tobacco smoke covered my taste buds, and filled my lungs, finding calm in the ritual. I felt a bit of a nicotine buzz hitting as I took my third drag, and I pulled out my phone to see that I had 3 text messages, two from Jenna.

Jenna: Osita is out of surgery and has opened her eyes. She pulled through!

Jenna: So I think I'm going to quit, and kidnap Osita. What do you think?

She had just been wine drunk and crying about how much she loved her job, what the fuck happened? The other text message came from an unknown number.

Unknown: You may know where the photos came from, and I feel guilty. I didn't mean to kill him, but I won't let you find me, not yet. Please know that I am sorry. I just meant to take his car out of commission. I truly am sorry. I should have turned myself in immediately, but I have kids, a family. I am so sorry

What the actual fuck?

I needed more information, whoever the fuck this was needed to give me a damn good explanation. I texted back the unknown number.

Me: Who is this?

The reply immediately came back:

Unknown: SERVICE ERROR 409: THE SUBSCRIBER YOU ARE TRYING TO REACH IS NO LONGER IN SERVICE.

Weird.

I can't believe I got a text from the person who murdered my father, and of course, they're too cowardly to respond, let alone allow me to message them back and discuss it like a real man. I wanted to punch him in the face, to rage and take out the years of anger and frustration on whoever the hell this was. This was not the way I expected to find out my father was murdered.

Eighteen

Jenna

My phone was ringing, so I answered.

"Jenna! Why am I hearing from your best friend that I need to call you and talk you down from the ledge, and that you have a *boyfriend*?! How dare you not tell your sister?!" Kristen screamed out over the phone. I held the handset at arms length and could just about tolerate the volume. I'm pretty sure a dog started barking a few houses down.

"Sorry, Kristen, it's been crazy lately. I was going to let you know as soon as I could, Osita just got hurt really bad and had surgery. I just... I just need a little break. Sorry I didn't let you know." I sighed. On the other end, I heard shuffling.

"Oh Jenny, I am so sorry. This was so selfish of me, I got too into my emotions. I am so sorry," she paused, "Wanna talk about it, sissy? It's always been us against the world."

I take a deep breath and exhale it slowly and stroke Osita's fur. "Yeah, why not. To answer your question, I started seeing

71

someone. His name is Damon West. We knew each other when we were younger. Remember when dad used to race? I guess not you were quite young. Anyway, he's tall, dark, and handsome," I laughed. "God, that sounds so cliche, but he is tall, at least six foot two, and he's *covered* in tattoos, mom's gonna hate that, and he's got dark hair, and honey colored eyes. He seems like he'd be a grump but there is nothing prettier than when he smiles. It's amazing." I giggled again.

"Sounds like someone has a little crush, but be careful, please. I have heard of him, and more to the point, I've heard he's bad news. He doesn't do serious sissy, and that's according to the town gossip."

The concern in her voice was hard to miss.

"When are you free? We have so much to catch up on," I changed the subject, knowing my sister it was better to have this conversation in person.

"I was actually going to call this evening to see if you'd go dress shopping with me this weekend?" I couldn't help but laugh.

"You've only been home for 24 hours, you can't wait to marry him can you?"

"Trust me if his mother wouldn't kill us for eloping we would have been married the day he proposed, that is, if it were up to me." she giggled.

Nineteen

Damon

"You good? You look like you saw a ghost."

Noah's voice ripped me from my thoughts.

"I just got a weird fucking message, someone claiming to be responsible for my dad's death. He swears that he didn't mean to kill him, and apparently he's feeling guilty but isn't ready for us to find him," I said, handing Noah my phone.

Noah stared at my phone in disbelief.

"We should reach out to someone who used to be on the Shear performance team," I went on, sighing as I ran my hand through my hair.

"Yeah, but who do we know that used to race with them, and is no longer associated with them?" Noah asked.

Inhaling deeply, Jenna's face filled my mind, "Donovan Moore, Jenna's dad." I replied. Hopefully, he'd be willing to talk to me. Jenna said he'd been not right for a while but she didn't give me a reason. I took my phone back from my best friend and called Jenna. She answered on the third ring, clearly puzzled why I was calling her during the workday.

"Hey Damon," her confused voice was adorable.

"Hey Kitten, I have a favor to ask," I said, not wanting to beat around the bush. "This is going to be a weird request, but do you think I could meet with your dad or have his number?"

"Um, I mean sure, but he will probably be extremely drunk, though you might have better luck if you go to The Stag, you know, the run-down bar on 28th? He's usually pretty deep in his cups by now over there." she said with a whimpering noise coming from the background.

"You're the best, and by the way, I was really glad to read Osita is doing well. As far as you wanting to kidnap her and quit, I'm sorry Kitten, but I don't think it's a smart decision. At least not as an immediate one without more consideration-"

"I know, I'm okay. I'm not actually gonna do it," she interrupted, "Emma told Kristen and I got an earful from her. I am not going to at least not yet. Good luck with talking to my dad. Even though I am not sure why you want to."

"Once I have more information I promise you'll be the first to know."

Twenty

Jenna

Not really sure why he wants to talk to my dad but maybe it has to do with racing.

I watched as Osita cuddled the stuffed animal and the blanket making whimpering noises while I gently stroked her fur.

"Don't worry sweetie, you're safe here. I will make sure of it, sweet girl," I promised. She attempted to chatter in response.

"Jenna, can we talk?" Dr. Jackson's voice cut in. I rolled my eyes down at Osita before turning and looking at him with a polite smile on my face.

"Yes, Dr. Jackson? Is there something I can help you with?"

"I wanted to apologize, it wasn't very professional, but I wanted to let you know that I do think you're brilliant, and you clearly care so much about the animals here, you're so considerate," he paused momentarily, "I overheard your phone call. You clearly have a boyfriend. If he ever does anything wrong will you please give me a chance to at least take you to lunch?" He watched my face expectantly for an expression.

"I mean I have someone I am seeing, and we work together. You're my superior. I don't think it would be a good idea."

"Well, it was worth a shot, but I have another thing I wanted to ask. Would you like to take Osita home tonight for observation? I know she'll be safe with you." His eyes fell on her. He wasn't wrong.

"Of course, I would love to. For the record, I don't think we'll be able to release her with the rest of her litter."

"I've been feeling for a while we more than likely wouldn't be able to, or possibly at all. So once she's healed we will have to potentially look for avenues to have someone adopt her." He responded.

I straightened up and adjusted my scrub top.

"That will hardly be necessary, I'll take her, for Pete's sake we know she trusts me, why stress her out more with multiple moves and new people? Where else could she stay with someone she knows and that can give her the best care?" I inquire, the scent of ammonia filling my nostrils.

"You really *are* the best candidate, I just didn't want you to feel like you *had* to take her.

Twenty-One

Damon

"Are you sure he's the right person to ask about this? I mean...
look, I know we all heard Jenna say he's a drunk. They
ain't exactly known for their reliability," Noah asked, leaning
forward between the driver and passenger seat.

"He's only in the sauce because Damon's dad was the closest
thing he had to a best friend. You ask me, he needs to get some
help and man the fuck up. He has Laura and them two girls to
take care of. They can't be any older than... what? Eighteen
and sixteen now?" George huffed.

I cocked my eyebrow at the grizzled old man.

"Uh George, Jenna is my age and her sister is two-year years
younger." I chuckled.

"Goddamnit, I am getting old." he huffed. The car came to a
halt outside the Stag. George looked at me and smirked.

"So, does this mean you're buying us a beer while we're on
the clock?" He winked at me. I shook my head in response.

"We're only here to get Donovan, sober him up, and ask him some questions. Understand?" I warned, eyeing George and Noah.

"Shit, with all the hooch Don's been drinking over the past ten years, his brain is more than likely floating in the stuff. I suspect it's gonna take at *least* a couple days for him to sober up." George said, looking at the front door and stroking his chin.

I rolled my eyes and, with a sigh, headed to the door and pulled it open, the bells tinkling, signaling to the barkeep that there were more people coming in to drink. The bar reeked of cheap beer, stale liquor, and old cigarette smoke. The old barkeep sleepily nodded at us before going back to lazily wiping a spotty glass with an equally spotty rag. I scanned the room taking in the place and allowing my eyes to adjust to the sudden darkness. When I looked back towards the end of the bar, I noticed a ragged disheveled man was sitting there. I felt George nudge me in my ribs.

"That's him. I'd know that ugly mug anywhere. You go on over, meet your girlfriend's dad and the only person who can help us. Noah and I will be sipping on a beer right... over here." he said, taking Noah by the shoulder and walking towards the bar to get their unauthorized beverages.

I felt my heart in my throat. Why was I so nervous? I took a deep breath and ran my hand through my hair. I walked over, sitting down beside Donovan.

"There are twenty *hic* empty seats. Why didn't you pick another seat? Or stay with your friends?" he rasped in between drinks of his beer.

"Well, I think you can help me out, Don," I responded, motioning for the barkeep to bring me a beer. He side eyed me.

"How could *I* be of any help? *Hic!*"

I took a sip of my lukewarm beer

"Don, what can you tell me about Miles West?" I asked cautiously, watching him out of my peripheral, and gauging his reactions.

"*Shiiiit.* I haven't heard that name in forever. *Hic!* He was the be- best fucking man I have *ever* known. *Hic.*" his voice started to trail off. He took a drink then got a far away look in his eyes.

"What- *hic* how do you know abou' Miles?" He slowly turned his face to me so he looked at me directly; there was a moment of clarity then his eyes started to tear up.

"Miles?" his voice cracked as if he was about to cry. It's true that I looked a lot like my father when he was my age though I am covered in tattoos.

"How?" his voice trailed off as his hand came up to my face.

"Don, I am Damon, his youngest son. I have some information about his death but I need you to be *sober* for that conversation. I, no, *we* need *your* help. Your wife and girls need you to sober up too. Do you think you can help us all?" I asked, placing my hand gently on the old man's shaky forearm.

"I-I Damon, I was the reason for his death. That stupid bet we had-" His voice quaked with guilt.

"If I hadn't taken him up on it- you, your brother and mother would still have your father-" he looked away but couldn't hide the quiet sobs. I opened my mouth to respond when George's voice interrupted me.

"Well Donovan, if you hadn't accepted his bet then you know he would have pestered you and probably would be haunting your ass right now. You and I both know that you both were always just so fucking competitive. He's glad you took the bet. Now we all need you to sober up and help us."

I was grateful I wasn't alone when we poured Donovan into the car. He kept sliding into Noah in the back seat, who did his best to keep him upright, and tried to avoid the fumes oozing off of him.

"You gonna be okay there Don?" Noah asked. He belched in response.

"Fuck's sake Don, you're gonna get the us all contact drunk with the stench comin off you." George said, rolling down the window and shifting in his seat uncomfortably.

Don, to his credit, managed to look a little embarrassed.

"Damon, how did you know where to find me?' he asked cautiously. I felt all their eyes on me, waiting for an answer. My knuckles turned white as I gripped the steering wheel tighter.

I cleared my throat. "Ah, well see about that, Donovon. I am sorta seeing your daughter," I said, adjusting and looking in the rearview mirror.

"You're dating Kristen?! Aren't you a little too old for her?" he asked.

George laughed out loud.

"Ah, no, Jenna, I am seeing Jenna. Kristen is um, she's engaged to a guy named Mark." I started trying to catch the man up as much as I personally could on some of the things that he had clearly missed in his own life. He probably wouldn't remember much of it,but I'd repeat it again and again if need be.

"You don't really seem Jenna's type," he started and paused briefly, "though that may be a good thing since those preppy bastards she normally goes for aren't good for her. They don't make her happy."

The burning in my chest told me I'd been holding my breath, and I let it out slowly. Hopefully, he was right.

I caught his eye in the mirror, "Hey, Don, you know you're going to have to lay off the sauce for a bit, right?" I cocked my eyebrow waiting on a response, he nodded slowly.

"Yeah, I'll try."

The rest of the drive was pretty quiet. Once we were back at the garage Noah and George got Donovan out of the back.

"Just take him to my office. There's a couch in there where he can rest and get him some water. A *lot* of water." I told them and turned to face the sound of running. Liam was jogging over, worry showing plain on his face.

"Hey man, there's some crazy shit happening." he said, looking around.

"Why what happened? What the fuck trouble did you get in to while I was gone?"

"There was someone here, but, like, there wasn't. I would see them then *poof* they were gone. It was like... I dunno, like they were a freaking ghost." He said, still looking around nervously.

It didn't make any sense for anyone to just show up to the garage. Our clients knew to always call before showing up so we could have someone available to walk them through their car. There was nothing that would pin dad's death on anyone in particular. Hell, the photographs we got from Greg didn't even do much good on that front either. We just knew what garage they came from.

"Alright, but you're ok? You didn't try to confront them did you?"

"No boss, I was keeping track of them on the cameras but it

was freaking weird. I didn't see them going over by any client cars, but it still felt shady as hell." Liam said.

Getting Don settled into the garage was easy enough. I thought he would pass out on the couch with a few bottles of water and a garbage can next to him, but it turned out that once he was actually in the garage, he wanted to see everyone's work. He followed George to his bay, and I nodded at him in passing as Noah and Liam followed me into my office. Liam tightened his bun anxiously as I took my seat behind my desk.

"Look, I'll be checking the cameras, man, don't worry. As long as you and Jax are okay, that's all that really matters to me. Well, besides the shop."

Noah looked between us both, his eyebrow slowly raising.

"What the hell did I miss?"

Liam just looked at me, nervous but steady. "You know me, boss, I ain't afraid to get rough, but this bastard just did not want to be seen. I kept spotting them just out of the corner of my eye. It was like I was seeing shit. Damon, I *know* I was *not*. Just. Seeing. Shit."

Noah just looked at me, waiting to be filled in.

"Liam caught someone on the cameras sneaking around the shop, it seemed he knew about where the cameras were at. Which tells *me* that they've done it before, but he just got noticed this time."

"No shit?" Noah exclaimed, his jaw dropping open.

"Yes shit, like I was saying, I'm going to be going over the security cam footage to get a better look at the guy."

"What do you think it means? Someone's going to try and rob us, or you think maybe someone found out we talked to Greg?"

I shrugged. "Maybe? We'll find out more once we look over

the footage."

I logged into my computer and pulled up the cameras. Noah and Liam moved to lean against the wall behind me. I pressed play, then fast forward through the "slow" parts, with our usual customers and business.

"Slow up boss, this was about the time I saw him. Maybe you'll recognize him, but I sure as fuck didn't."

As it turned out, a figure I'd never seen before popped up on the screen. I'd almost let the video scroll by before I hit pause and went back a few frames, focusing in on the mystery figure.

"Liam, I know you said you only saw him through your peripheral, but is this the guy?"

He nodded. "Yeah boss, that's him, I'm sure. I went out there to talk to him but he high-tailed out of there."

And of fucking course, there were no decent shots of his face.

He was clearly looking for dad's car. I watched as he skulked, heading to the spot where it normally sat, but it was currently in a bay. Liam clearly spooked him, and he ran off, Liam popping into frame trying to get a better look at where the mystery figure went. I don't blame the guy for bolting, Liam looks menacing as fuck, but to those who know him, he's actually a giant teddy bear.

"I'm sorry I didn't catch him, Damon. It was just really unexpected."

"Don't worry man, I know you would've if you could've."

"Shit, Liam, he probably felt your big ass stomping over to him and thought it was a T-rex." Noah said with a laugh, clapping the big man on the back.

The video left us with more questions than answers, but one thing was clear. The next morning I was definitely going to go have a talk with the owner of Shear Performance.

Twenty-Two

Jenna

I made my rounds at the end of the day, making sure that I was getting everything I would need to see Osita through the night. I was grabbing a few extra bandages when there was a noise behind me so I slowly turned around; expecting Dr. Jackson. Instead it was Susan, clutching a clipboard to her chest while she looked at me and the tiny kit in the cage sympathetically.

"How is she doing?" she asked, her voice barely above a whisper.

Smiling at her gently I open the cage, "She has a long way to go but she is quite the little fighter, tonight she is coming home with me. Dr. Jackson's orders. Then she'll be here every day that I am working so I can keep an eye on her," I rub Osita's back gently, "We both appreciate your concern, don't we little one?"

Osita chirped softly in response and gently curled by my finger.

Susan looked away, "I am sorry this even happened Jenna, really, if there is anything I can do to help please let me know." she said, clutching the clipboard tighter to her chest. She brought her gaze back to us with a small frown.

I nod "There is one thing you can do. When you find the people responsible, make sure they can't neglect any other animals like this."

Susan looked a bit shocked by my directness, but then she nodded and walked away quickly. I turned around to get the carrier ready for the weak kit's trip back to my house. A cough interrupted my adding blankets and snuggle buddies to the carrier, I turned to see both Dr. Thomas and Dr. Jackson.

I exhaled slowly.

"Hello doctors, I finished my rounds and am getting Osita ready for her trip, isn't that right pretty girl?"

Dr Jackson smiled at me and the kit. "Good, I am glad that she is going to a place where she will receive the proper attention she should have received last night."

"Oh can it Daniel," Dr. Thomas snapped quickly before he could catch himself. He closed his eyes and followed by resignedly saying, "She will be safe at your place tonight Jenna, you are truly a gifted vet tech. Very smart and perceptive."

"Wow, thank you, Dr. Thomas, that means a lot coming from such a talented vet, if only your personality matched. Now if you'll excuse me gentlemen, I need to finish getting Osita ready to leave."

"Right, uh, well we'll leave you to it," Dr. Thomas stumbled over his words, turning to walk away awkwardly.

Hopefully to find some burn cream...

"Hey, Jenna, if you need anything and I mean *anything* with Osita or whatever, call me I'll answer no matter the time." Dr.

Jackson said, genuine concern in his voice.

I bundled Osita up, said my goodbyes, and the two of us made for home.

Getting Osita settled was pretty easy since she had her crate and was surrounded by familiar and comforting smells. I hated that I had to feed her with a syringe to her mouth, but I knew the food would help comfort her, and I also knew that no matter how familiar the scents, she was scared to be in a new place away from her gaze. After she finished eating, she nestled down to sleep in my lap, knowing that I was a safe space.

I debated calling or texting Damon but I wasn't sure if he'd answer or not. More than that, I couldn't shake the feeling I was rushing into this. I mean, I had only really known him for a short time. Yes, I felt something with him that I had never felt with anyone before, but I needed to get myself under control. I needed to give him space to do his own thing. Hell, I needed to focus on *Osita*, not *some guy*. Not some... dark-haired, eyes almost like midnight, tattoo-covered, crooked smiled, bad boy. I shivered. Maybe it was indigestion.

I mean, I didn't even know if he was a good man. While I mused on my gut feelings, I continued gently stroking Osita until I felt her breathing slow and I could tell she was sleeping peacefully. I gently lay her back in her carrier and shut the door, before going to continue meal prepping for the next week. I was in the middle of chopping vegetables when my cell phone buzzed on the counter, rudely silencing the music that had been softly playing in the background.

Emma's name blazoned across the screen as I picked up the phone to answer. She didn't even wait for me to say hello before starting to talk at a mile a minute.

"Oh my god, this week has been the *longest*. How is Osita? Damon? Work? *Me*? My life is a *mess*, Ricky called it off. *Again*. Not that it's a surprise to *anyone*." She took a quick breath before continuing. "Do you remember Sean, the partner at my law firm? Well, apparently he is starting his own firm. He can't take being a partner to Everett anymore. And in case you were wondering, Sean's the thirty-two-year-old, not the old man. I digress. This could change so many things, Jen! Enough about me! What's been new with you?"

"Goodness, that was... *a lot* to take in. Starting with the Ricky news, you deserve so much better than that pompous douche canoe. As far as Sean is concerned, what do you think is going to happen next? And as far as what's going on with me... Osita is home with me, with my work's blessing, don't worry, and then there's Damon. I don't know Emma..." I released a sigh. "He asked about my dad and where to find him. I just- I don't know what's going on in his head from one minute to the next, and I for sure don't know what's with me and how I feel about him."

"Well, that sucks. Boys are *stupid* Jenna, we need to do away with them."

"I feel like there's a few people that would frown on that sort of thing. Cops for one, society at large for another. Your employer, possibly."

"Ugh... *stupid* rules for *stupid* boys. Oh well, I'll have to find another way."

I stopped her before she could continue.

"Em, I've actually got a more serious question... if I knew who was behind Osita getting hurt but she's being protected by one of the owners, what would be the best course of action for me to take?"

She thought for a second, before continuing on in her most lawyer tone of voice. "If you don't have hard evidence, then I probably wouldn't say anything. If you do, however, you should tell them what you know. They will most likely be corroborating your story by reviewing the evidence, but if it came to light that you knew something untoward was happening and chose *not* to share it, it could reflect badly on you. Especially in a small environment like that. You don't need to make some public declaration, but letting the other owner or owners know *what* you know would be the most beneficial course of action, I think."

For the next few weeks, every day that Em wasn't dealing with Ricky, she was at my house with me and Osita. I barely heard from Damon. I didn't really know what was going on, but I didn't feel that I knew him well enough to press. My mom had barely heard or seen from my father as well, but that wasn't unheard of. He'd get drunk, disappear for a day or four and then just reappear as if nothing had happened.

This time, Damon claimed he had my father and that he was safe, whatever that meant. I was afraid. I was afraid that Damon was sliding down a slippery slope with my alcoholic father either in tow or leading the way. I couldn't tell which of those ideas was worse. It made me nervous. I noticed that Em paused the movie or show that I forgot we were even watching. I looked over at her to see her staring at me. "Welcome back! I thought we lost you to the mines."

I blinked at her.

"Mines- I- What? What are you talking about?"

"Oh you were so deep in your head I thought you must have been spelunking. I was going to go get a rescue team if you didn't come up soon."

"I wasn't 'deep in my head,' as you say, I just spaced out for a second, thats all!

"Bullshit Jen. I know you better than anyone and if you *were* in the present moment with me you would have pointed out the plot holes. At least five of them so far. Also I literally paused the movie five minutes ago, what is going on inside that pretty little head of yours?"

I fidgeted with my shirt.

"It's stupid. I haven't heard from Damon much this week, and he's been spending a lot of time with my dad. *Him* I know, and I just… I'm almost starting to feel like maybe that's why he decided to keep talking to me, or… I don't know Em, I said it was stupid."

She grabbed my hand and squeezed it gently. "It's not stupid, honey. The years with Ricky have taught me it's not worth getting all depressed over some guy. Let's get dolled up and go dancing, okay?"

We raided my closet as Osita chattered from her bed in the middle of my bed. Just before we walked out the door, I gave her a little kiss and put her into her cage so she couldn't hurt herself why we were away. The last thing I wanted to do was go out, but I couldn't let down my best friend. Maybe she was right, maybe I needed to put Damon on the back burner and have a little fun. Once we were in the car, I silenced my phone and slid it into my purse.

Once inside, we grabbed a couple drinks; then headed out to the dance floor. The music was blasting from the speakers; the bass punching through us, and so we started dancing, and I felt myself having fun in spite of myself. I'd only finished half my drink when I started to feel dizzy, but I figured it was due to not eating much today, the alcohol seeping into my system, and now dancing a lot.

Fuck it.

Despite feeling dizzy, I kept drinking my drink and kept up the dancing. I wondered where Emma had got to and looked over my shoulder for her, and that's when I saw Dr. Thomas approaching.

"Jenna?"

Ugh... gross.

"Um, hi. What's up Doc, fanshy meeting you in a plashe like this." My tongue was feeling heavy, I wanted to rest it.

He laughed in reply, "Please, no need to be so formal here, Archer will do fine. Why don't we get somewhere a little more private so we can talk."

"Wait Doc- Archer. I'm wif my-"

Before I could find and signal to Emma, he had tugged me over to a secluded area.

"I knew I recognized you, Jenna. God*damn*, don't you look beautiful." Dr. Thomas, Archer was practically on top of me, way closer than I was comfortable with. My head was starting to swim. Archer was scruffy, with gray running through the uneven stubble on his face, leering at me with hungry eyes. I knew he was trying to flirt with me, but where Damon oozed charm, Archer just... oozed. Like an infection. I couldn't help but feel uncomfortable, so I tried to shift away from him.

"Thanksh, doc, but I'm here wif my bes frien." My words felt weird, my tongue felt heavier than it used to. I think. I raised my arm to wave, or tried to, but he caught it and brought it back down.

He smirked at me, and my skin crawled. I tried to turn away from him. Why couldn't he bother someone else? And why do I feel so fuckin' dizzy? He squeezed my arm and tugged me into him.

"Well, I didn't see you with anyone. I just saw you. Come on, let me get you another drink, beautiful, you look thirsty."

I tried to open my mouth to protest, but nothing came out.

I would've swore I saw Damon as the whole world went black around me.

Twenty-Three

29 Damon

"Thank fucking god, I need a drink after all, well, fucking everything." Noah griped into his whiskey while the music blared from the dance floor behind us.

I knew what he meant, I'd agreed to go out with Noah after the long ass week we all had. Few weeks, in fact. We'd been trying to get a meeting with the owner of Shear Performance since Don came to us, but it was like pulling teeth. Every day brought new excuses and no answers or guarantees. On top of that, keeping an eye on Don was getting a bit ridiculous, I hadn't even talked to Jenna much during the week and it had been eating at me. I downed my whiskey and swirled glass around the bar, watching as it turned back and forth. I let out a sigh.

"Since when do you sigh? Especially when you're here?" Noah asked, eyeing me suspiciously. "Gonna order a cranberry juice next?"

When I looked up to answer him, I saw Jenna in the mirror and my heart nearly jumped out of my chest. She was being tugged down that little hallway where she'd willingly gone with me. There was some dickhead holding her by the arm, and she looked like they were talking close... but my gut told me something was off. I crossed the dance floor, watching as she tried to reject this asshole when she looked me dead in my eyes, just before hers rolled back in her head. I shoved the lecherous prick aside and caught my girl before she fell, gently setting her in a chair. I whistled signaling to Noah to come to us before rounding back on *him*.

"What the *fuck* did you do to her, asshole?"

"I didn't do anything to her, *pal*. Now if you don't mind, I was about to take my date home, so why don't you fuck off back to your *boyfriend*."

"See that's the problem. I do mind. Just so happens that's *my* girl right there, and no means *no* asshole."

Noah entered the hall just as my fist made contact with his nose and before his head bounced off the wall with a hollow thump we could hear over the music. Blood poured down his face and chest as he slumped to the floor, and before I could follow him to continue the beating, Noah pushed me off and against the wall.

"Jesus fucking christ! Damon!" Noah looked at me then over at Jenna slumped in the chair. "What the fuck happened?"

I looked past Noah and saw the girl that Jenna was with the first night we reconnected. Emma, if I remembered right. Jenna had talked about her a few times, and she was at her house that night I picked her up. I silently made a mental note that I needed to learn Jenna's friends names after we got her out of here. She blanched and let out a shocked squeak as she saw the pale form of her best friend slumped in the chair and a man with blood covered khakis holding his nose and cursing me for breaking it.

"You shut the fuck up with your whining before I hit you again." I growled, rage making me want to plaster this fuck all over the wall. "Noah, call our sheriff friend. Emma isn't it?" The brunette nodded at me, her mouth agape in shock. I nodded back at her and tried to steady my voice. "Thank you, and I need you to do me a favor. Can you take Jenna to the hospital? And take whatever she was drinking with you. I think douchecanoe here drugged her, or had a friend at the bar do it."

"I didn't fucking touch her, man, you got the wrong guy!"

"Buddy, I fucking promise you that you're going to want to keep your mouth shut until the cops get here or you might not have the teeth left to tell your story. Damon. DAMON! I've fucking got him, get Jenna to Emma's car!"

I didn't realize I'd already pulled the greasy fuck to his feet before I felt Noah's grip on my cocked arm, and I opened my clenched fist to let go of his shirt.

"Fine. *I'm fine*, Noah. Keep an eye on this prick while I take her."

"You already know I will, now GO!"

I scooped Jenna into my arms, my kitten laying limp against my chest as the crowd parted from in front of us. I walked out of the bar to find Emma pulling up in front, Jenna's unfinished drink in the cup holder. I carefully set Jenna in Emma's front seat before kissing the side of her head and buckling her in.

"Drive fast, but careful Emma. I'll be by as soon as I can with everything going on here."

95

Twenty-Four

Jenna

Beeping.

What was all that beeping?

Why did my head hurt so bad? God I'm so sleepy...

My eyes drifted open to the sight of fluorescent lights and machines in a room that smelled like disinfectants.

Oh fuck, how much did I even drink...

There was a doctor talking to Emma in the corner. Her eyes were rimmed red and glossy like she'd been crying. And up all night. She gestured and looked over at me, and so I went to wave at her. It was so weak.

God, I hadn't felt like this in years. My twenty-first wasn't even this bad.

"Jen, hey! You're awake!" She ignored whatever the doctor was saying to her and shushed him with a raised hand before almost running over to me. "Girl, you scared the hell out of me!"

I let out a soft chuckle and croaked out "I'm sorry, Em."

"Make sure you check in with me the next time you decide to get roofied, ok?"

"Is that what happened? I- I don't remember much, Just dancing with you and things starting to get fuzzy."

She clasped my hand and gave it a squeeze before grabbing a water bottle out of her purse. The doctor cocked his eyebrow at her.

"After what she's been through tonight," she said, cracking open the bottle, "There is no way I am letting her drink tap water. She *deserves* bottled water."

She gingerly placed the bottle to my lips.

"I'm going to make some rounds and be back, but we need to talk more about what happened last night, miss," the doctor stated from the foot of my bed, "You're a lucky young lady to have a friend that was able to take care of you and get you here so quickly."

"That's what I've been trying to tell her for years, doc." Emma said in a sweet sing song voice. I groaned softly against the water bottle in response, nearly choking.

"Oops, sorry, I haven't had to be the one to hold a water bottle to your lips since your twenty-first." she said, tucking a strand of my hair behind my ear like my mom used to when I was little, I placed my hand on hers. She was trembling. I noticed the doctor had quietly made his exit.

"Emma, what happened? Why don't I don't remember?"

For once she was the one chewing on her lip nervously when we both heard a knock at the door and she jumped up protectively. I hadn't seen her be like this since high school. She opened her mouth to answer, but just then Damon opened the door. Slowly. And with my father and mother, sister and her fiance following behind him and some dirty blond haired guy I had never seen before. I was clearly not the only one to take in the visitors. Emma was busy eyefucking the blond that brought up the tail and was unaware of my growing panic. He whispered something to Damon before patting him on the shoulder and turning around to leave.

"Hey Kitten," his voice was rough, and his bruised hand hung laxly at his side. Something in me clicked. I was scared of him. *Why?*

I started shaking. I couldn't see him like this, I couldn't. I didn't want to see him. I didn't want him here. I didn't want him here. I didn't want him here at all. He had to leave. I needed him out of here now.

"Get out! *Get out* now Damon!" I shouted through hot tears streaming down. His eyes widened in surprise and hurt, but he nodded at me.

"I… K-Kit… Ok, I'm leaving."

"Jen…" Emma trailed off as he left the room quickly, and the door closed on whatever we were or were going to be.

Twenty-Five

Damon

What the fuck was that? What did I do? Was it because I brought Don with us?

A million thoughts raced through my mind as I walked through the halls of the hospital back to the entrance. I stepped outside to go to my car, and saw Noah was standing by my door checking his phone and trying to light a cigarette. When he looked up at my approach, I could see the recognition turn to confusion in his eyes. Frustrated, I just shook my head at him. The last thing I wanted now was questions I didn't have the answers to. He simply put the cig back in the pack and slipped into the unlocked passenger door before I gunned it out of the parking lot.

I needed a drink. I needed a few of them. I wanted to hit something. Again. I wanted to rage and yell and fight and fuck and I wanted none of it if she wasn't going to go with me, if she wasn't going to continue with us. I knew this was all still new but goddamnit I wanted this girl in my life. I'd hardly wanted anything more and as the miles clicked by that future felt further and further away.

I headed back to the bar. Where it all had gone down a few hours before. I ordered my whiskey neat, as always, but this time I didn't stop after two. At four glasses in, I saw a familiar face saunter towards me. It took everything I had to not roll my eyes.

"What the fuck do you want Nikki?" There was nothing in the rulebook that said I had to be nice to her. I think.

She gasped, but still kept coming toward me with a cloyingly sweet smile. I tried to not let my skin crawl off my body.

"Wooow, someone is as cheerful as ever! You know... I think I know just how I can make your night better." She purred, planting her hands on my chest and slithering closer to me, tilting her face up for a kiss.

"No. Thanks." I bit out.

"Well, why the hell not? Your little *princess* is nowhere to be found," she stamped her foot like a toddler. "Hell she probably won't be around. Who would have thought the daughter of the town fuckin' drunk was a druggie. *Everyone* saw what happened when you punched Archer in the face."

Good, maybe they'll think twice before they try anything like that again. Wait, what the hell did she mean-

My eyebrows knitted in confusion and anger.

"Why do you seem so confused Damon, that is what happened *right*? She took too many drugs and overdosed *right*? Archer was telling everyone all about it right before he went to check on her." She scoffed, shaking her head like she pitied me.

I stepped back away from her, my back bumping against the

bar. I *never* would hit a woman, but I could feel myself losing control.

Why would someone spread that rumor about sweet, innocent Jenna? And just who the fuck was this Archer guy?

As I was about to push past Nikki and try to walk away from the situation I caught a flash of movement over Nikki's shoulders. That flash turned out to be Emma, who took the opportunity to throw a drink squarely in Nikki's face. Her look of surprise and shock left her looking like a soaked blowup doll, and I had to stop myself from laughing in her face.

"Listen here, you two faced slut, my *best* friend was drugged by your *good* friend Archer. I know for an absolute *fact* she's only smoked weed once, but if you want to continue to run your mouth and spread bullshit rumors about her, then I'll make sure we sue you for slander. Matter of fact, don't let me stop you, I'll just go ahead and record you saying them. You don't mind being on tape, right? I thought not, you seem like that kind of… girl."

Nikki went from an indignant wet hen to looking like she'd seen a ghost faster than I'd ever driven, and she high tailed it out of the bar and into the night she came from.

My mouth was agape, speechless.

"Holy shit Emma," I finally chuckled. "That was amazing. Wait, why are you here? Shouldn't you be over at the hospital? What happened?!" Emma just smiled sadly and my heart sank again.

"Oh no, oh my god, she was ok-"

A look of panic flashed across Emma's face.

"No! Oh my gosh, no, nothing like that, she's ok. But she did have a massive panic attack and I don't know why. The doctors gave her something to take that edge off, but it seems like you might be a trigger for her."

"How could that be? We haven't spoken much these last couple weeks, but I didn't think I'd done anything that bad. We've been working with her dad and trying to keep an eye on him and looking into everything about my dad and there was someone trying to-"

She put her hand up, silencing me with the gesture.

"Slow down sweetie, you were dangerously close to a drunken ramble."

"Yes ma'am." I said sheepishly.

"Good boy. Now, I don't think it was anything you did per se, but she's coming out of a traumatic event and she was just waking up. That said, I think it would be best for her if you stayed away for a little while."

"That's…" I nearly shouted at her, but sense took over at the last moment, "fine, ok."

She nodded slowly. "Good. Good, thank you for understanding, Damon. Let her come to you, if anything, and for what it's worth from me, thank you for being there tonight. Bet you don't get called a knight in shining armor often."

"Ha, no, no I don't think anyone's ever accused me of that before."

"Well, you were tonight. Get home safe boys."

She gave me one last sad smile and left with a lingering look at the two of us. I watched her leave before collapsing back into the barstool.

"Son of a bitch." I said exasperatedly. Noah put his hand on my shoulder and squeezed reassuringly.

"I know man, I know. Don't worry, I'm sure she'll come around eventually." He held up his hand to signal the bartender for another whiskey for me and water for himself.

Of all the ways I thought this night would go, this would never have occurred to me.

Twenty-Six

Jenna

My ears picked up the beeping of machines, and gently hushed whispers. I kept my eyes closed as I thought through what that meant and came to the conclusion that what I'd just gone through, that weird hospital dream where Damon showed up with my family in tow actually happened.

Oh nooo... No Damon, what did I do to you? What had I said...

I felt a weight on my chest that I thought was sorrow until I realized it was an actual softly snoring and fuzzy weight. My eyes fluttered open to see Osita sleeping peacefully on me, her carrier not in sight.

"Hey sleepy girl," I said softly to her, "Did you convince someone that you're an emotional support puppy?"

"Jenna, you're awake! She was having a tough time without you at the house, and I figured you'd both need some support when you woke up so I smuggled her in. I figured with her little bandit mask, she wouldn't be opposed to a little crime.

I'm sorry, did we wake you?" Emma said, turning to face me from where she'd been talking quietly with Kristen.

"She's too young to be involved in your scheming!" I said while idly stroking her head and back.

"It's never too early to start honing your craft, that's what I say. She has a long life of breaking and entering and theft to look forward to. I'm just being a good aunt and helping her along." Her chest rose with apparent pride and I laughed.

"Anyone ever tell you you'd make a good lawyer?" Kristen said with a crooked smile.

"My parents, when I was a child, *just* look at me now."

Osita started chattering annoyedly at all this noise interrupting her nap, then more excitedly when she realized I was petting her.

Emma and Kristen both rushed over and tried to hush her.

"Oh, Osita, you gotta be quiet, sweetie. They'll kick you out if they know you're here!" Emma begged the kit. I stifled a giggle sitting up slowly, raising the bed to meet my back since I still felt a little lightheaded from last night. Osita climbed up my chest and was nestling against my neck and shoulder when a knock came at the door.

Kristen and Emma looked at me with panic but Osita scrambled along to hide behind my neck. I tried very hard not to react to the feel of her tiny paws tickling me as the nurse came into the room, accompanied by what I assumed was the doctor.

They explained to me that I had been drugged and asked if there was anything I remember. I told them about showing up to the bar, getting the drink and starting to feel strange after dancing a little, but I'd thought it was from not eating earlier.

"Miss, I have to ask, is there anything you took that we

should know about. We've pumped your stomach and so far it seems like your story matches up, but if there's medication, or something you took recreationally, it could affect your treatment going forward. For now, we've had you on plenty of fluids since you came in."

"Nothing Doctor, I'm not on any meds and the only thing I do recreationally is maybe a drink or two with friends. I don't even smoke weed."

He nodded, "That lines up with what your friend and mother had to say. We're going to keep monitoring you for now, but for what it's worth, it's my medical opinion that someone slipped you something last night. Hopefully our tox screen comes back soon and we can give you some more answers. For now, rest up and be careful, ok?"

We all thanked the doctor and the nurse recorded my vitals into my chart before following him out the door. Osita poked her head out around my neck to make sure the coast was clear before nuzzling into my shoulder and neck again.

"Sooo, um, are we going to actually discuss what happened last night or is everyone going to act like someone died?"

Kristen and Emma shared a sympathetic look. Emma cleared her throat. And Kris sat gently on the side of my bed and squeezed my hand as I did to hers more times than I could count growing up.

"Archer." Emma stated briefly.

Apparently the confusion was all over my face.

"Archer, he drugged you, or the bartender did. I didn't even realize you were separated from me until I noticed Damon rushing across the dance floor."

Kris squeezed my hand again, smiling at me.

"Then... what happened with Damon?"

"Damon came to your rescue. He confronted Archer and hurt his hand by punching him in the nose, sissy." Kristen's normal boisterous voice was soft and barely a whisper. Emma nodded, confirming what she must have already told Kristen.

My face and heart fell. "I fucked up…" my voice trailed off and I could feel a lump forming in my throat.

Emma climbed in on the other side of me and my sister moved so all three of us were cuddled together with the kit on my cheek in the hospital bed. Hot tears streamed down my face and a choked sob escaped my throat.

"Hey, hey, hey, it's ok now Jen. You were scared and you'd just woken up. He understands, I promise. Or at least, he will. It'll be okay. I went and talked to him after you passed out again." They cuddled me closer when we heard the door handle jiggle. We all jumped slightly. Osita scampered back to her hiding place just as the door opened to reveal Mark with 3 coffees in hand and some flowers in a vase. He looked at us from the door handle puzzled and concerned.

"Bad time?" He looked like he was about to back out the door until his eyes met my sister's and she greeted him with a smile.

"No babe, it's okay. We were just talking and cuddling."

Later that day I was released. After I got home and had Osita situated again, I tried countless times to call Damon but to no avail. I couldn't shake the feeling, despite Emma and Kristen's reassurance, that I'd really messed things up with Damon. I felt bad for taking what happened out on him like that, but … well, I don't know. I just hoped that he would get back to me soon.

I decided to try and put it out of my mind by taking a hot bath to try and relax, as well as wash the hospital off of me. Still,

I spent that night tossing and turning fitfully, until I finally gave in to a restless sleep, and woke late the next morning.

Since I was feeling better, I decided to take advantage of it and take Osita to the clinic while no one was around to check her vitals and make sure everything was on track with her healing process. I made sure her carrier had some clean bedding and a little cat toy for her to play with, then bundled her up and headed into the clinic.

I pulled into the parking lot and noticed that Susan's car was in the lot. I said a silent prayer to whoever was listening that I'd be able to get in and out without being noticed, opened the door and headed inside.

I had just finished recording Osita's temp and was trying to listen to her heart when she started chattering excitedly.

"Osita, you gotta hold still baby I'll get you a treat later, but right now-"

"She's being a little squirrely for a raccoon, huh?"

I damn near jumped out of my skin at hearing Susan's voice right behind me like that. I heard her giggling and trying to apologize after I got my heart to go back into my chest.

"I'm ha, I'm sorry Jenna, I promise I didn't mean to startle you! Are you alright?" her amusement had faded to a gentle concern.

"I'm fine Susan, it's alright. I just didn't hear you come in and I was so focused and- I'm fine. How're you doing?"

She raised an eyebrow at my question. "Shouldn't I be asking you that? Your friend, the lawyer, let us know what happened. I thought you'd be at home resting and taking some time."

I could feel myself flush at the response. "I'm ok, really. And honestly, I was going a little stir crazy, and Osita needed her vitals checked, so I figured I'd get us out of the house and kill two birds with one stone."

I shrugged; it felt like a lame answer and I was more than a little embarrassed at what happened, but I couldn't put my finger on why. I guess that it happened at all, but I wasn't used to being fussed over ever.

How many times am I going to have this conversation?

"Well, I'm glad to hear you're feeling better at least. You can take as much time as you need, but I know that we, and the rest of our patients, are looking forward to you being back on."

"Thank you, Susan. I really appreciate everyone letting me take some time and get my head around this."

"Of course. Let me know if there's anything I can do for you or our little friend here." Susan said, not knowing what I knew about her conversation with Carly.

I should speak up...

"Actually, Susan, there is one big thing you can do for me, for her, really."

"Oh? What's that?"

"You need to talk to Amara about what you know happened. I overheard you talking with Carly in the hall the other day, so I know you know what led to Osita getting hurt. I don't care about their affair, as inappropriate as it is they're both adults to make up their own minds. What I *do* care about is that their carelessness led directly to one of our patients nearly dying. You *need* to tell Amara."

Susan's jaw dropped in surprise at what I said, but she regained her composure, and nodded thoughtfully.

"Thank you, Jenna. I'd... I'd honestly not looked at it in that light, but you're right."

I snuck back out to my car, got Osita situated and was

startled yet again by Daniel sidling up to my window.

"Jenna!"

For the love of- is there some ninja class I missed for this clinic?

"Gah! I mean, sorry, hello Daniel."

"I thought that was your car, aren't you supposed to be resting."

"I know, I've heard, but Osita needed her vitals drawn and I was going crazy at home." I said, fidgeting awkwardly with the steering wheel.

"Well, I sure hope they find the bastard that drugged you. Who would have ever thought that something like that would happen in our small town?"

I plastered on a blank grin as I tried not to let my emotions get me. I clenched my hands into fists, digging my nails into my palms, and causing me to focus on the pain.

If he noticed my uneasiness, he didn't show it as he continued on unabated, "Did you hear Dr. Thomas picked up kickboxing? Apparently, in his first class, he got ass handed to him! He had to get 6 stitches and his nose broke!"

I stifled a laugh.

So that's the story he was going with for everyone. Wouldn't want your coworkers to know what a fucking creep you are, would you?

I couldn't help but wonder what happened from the time I started to now.

When I first started, he was so devoted to Amara and caring for animals, always ready to help anywhere and everywhere needed. He was passionate about care and would have meetings every month about ways to improve the patient and client experience.

"Jenna? Hey, are you sure you're good to drive?"

I blinked and shook my head yes, "Yeah, sorry Daniel, I

was just thinking how incredible it is that a man of his age is willing to take up such a *physical* activity without experience, or without being medicated."

I smiled more brightly at him, trying to shake off his concerns. Osita chirped in annoyance from her carrier in the passenger seat.

"Oh, I am so sorry miss ma'am, did we wake you?" I asked, turning my attention to her.

"How has she been doing?" His voice was soft, I noticed that he drew his lips together. I smiled and gently pulled her out of the carrier and sat her in my lap. His fingers scratched under her chin and she mewled for him. He smiled warmly at her little noises.

"Wonderful, truly. She has been healing extremely well. She's a tough little girl, I just wanted to check her vitals to confirm everything."

He nodded, his blue eyes reflecting the sunshine.

Since Damon wasn't answering my phone calls, and I had already basically decided to quit the clinic an idea formed in my head. The only thing keeping me there was that I needed to make sure I had adopted Osita so they couldn't take her away from me.

I did the unthinkable.

"Say, Daniel, would you like to grab coffee with me?"

"Oh, sure Jenna! This is a surprise, though. I would be delighted to, but I can't today. Would tomorrow morning be okay?" His eyes flashed a sadness and hopefulness in the same moment.

I nodded. "I have a doctor's appointment at eight, but just let me know what time works best for you."

I pulled a napkin and a pen from my glove compartment,

and quickly jotted down my digits and handed it to him.
"Thanks, Jenna. I'll be calling you."

Twenty-Seven

Damon

I didn't know what to do with myself.

The rest of that night I got so drunk I don't even remember getting home, but I woke up on my couch, with a bucket next to me, along with two bottles of water and five ibuprofen. I don't know if it was Noah or if past Damon decided to be nice to me, but I had a feeling it was Noah. Current Damon though felt like he deserved the punishment, even though he wasn't sure just what the fuck he did to deserve it in this case.

Damon needed to stop thinking in the third person before his head really did split open.

I sat up, s l o w l y, and let my world settle back down into one plane as opposed to doing all that swimming and sloshing around. Once I was confident that I wouldn't actually need the bucket, I cracked open one of the bottles of water and took a small sip, then another, and finally a long drink along with all the ibuprofen. I finished off the rest of the water bottle before grabbing the other one and leaning back against the couch, closing my eyes and pressing the cool bottle to my forehead.

Fuck me, why'd I drink that much... Oh, because I felt my future slipping away, that's right.

I scoffed at my own thoughts then winced in pain. I needed to do something, anything more than just lying here in my own misery trying not to be sick.

Alright Damon, we can do this. On the count of three. Ready? One...

I stood up and held on to the couch to make sure I didn't fall over. Once my equilibrium came back, again, I slowly made my way to the bathroom, water bottle in hand.

I turned the shower on to cool and stood inside for a moment, letting the water cascade over me while I leaned against the wall. I cracked open the second bottle of water and started drinking while the shower poured over me. Eventually, I felt enough of my strength and will to live return that I was able to turn the water to warm and actually wash. I wrapped a towel around my waist and headed to my room to get dressed, found my wallet, phone, and keys, then headed over to the shop to channel my feelings into something else.

It took me so long to get out of bed and the house that it was already afternoon by the time I got in. It was just after I'd set up that I realized I'd never actually checked my phone since this morning, and after scrolling through my missed calls, I found that Jenna had called. A lot.

I set my phone down, and slid under the Camaro.

If she wanted me to stay away I'd do just that. Who was I kidding? I wasn't good enough for her anyway.

That's when I heard George and Don enter the garage talking about what happened over the weekend.

"I don't know George, you should have seen the way she looked at him. It was like she saw a ghost. She was terrified, started shakin' and screaming for him to get out of there."

I held my breath and quit turning the wrench to try and listen in. Waiting to see where the conversation was headed.

"Well Don, I mean, she was drugged and you said she couldn't remember anything, except seeing him and then black. Hell, I can't imagine anyone would be too brave after that. Ah, Morning Liam, Jax, Noah. How're you ladies doing this fine day?"

Shit.

I knew that meant the end of them talking, but I knew that there was nothing I could do to change her mind. I just needed to focus on finding out who caused my dad's accident. I rolled the creeper out from under the Camaro.

"Hey guys, meeting in the conference room in 20 minutes!" I shouted, regretted it immediately, and wiped my hands on a towel while walking toward my office. Racing season was quickly approaching, and we were getting busier and busier. If we wanted to be able to take care of our clients, and our cars, we needed to get on schedule along with figuring out the next plans.

I felt my heart breaking a little more, so I texted April to send me a picture of my niece and was pulled out of my pity party when a knock came at my door.

"Yeah?" I gruffed.

"Hey man, you holdin' up okay? You had a shit weekend." Noah said, not fully coming into my office which wasn't like him.

I gave him a half-assed shrug and was about to speak when a throat-clearing interrupted. Garrett, our sheriff friend, was behind him, and judging by the look on his face I wasn't going to like what he had to say.

I waved them both in and indicated the chairs across from my desk. Both men had a seat and sat there looking long-faced, I was wondering how long this would go on when Garrett broke the silence first, "Damon, I have bad news, there is no evidence that that guy drugged your girl."

I clenched my hands tightly into a fist and fought the flash of white hot rage that rose inside me.

"He's smart and shifty. Of course there wasn't." I bit out.

"I tried everything in my power to hold him until we could find something, but we couldn't. From there, he decided against pressing charges. Against you. Says he understands how it must've looked from your perspective, and while rash, he probably would've done the same. I still think he looks good for doing it, but we just don't have anything to go on. Nothing on Jenna's tox report, nothing on the cameras until he pulled her aside and you went after him. I'm sorry, man." I nodded at the man who, ever since I could remember, had been all about justice. Even when I was at my lowest he and Noah *always* tried to pull me out of the dark. I was fully convinced he became a cop just so he could keep me out of trouble.

I was annoyed, and frustrated as all hell, but if Garett said there was nothing he could do, he meant it.

Fuck. Thanks for looking into it man. Keep in touch if anything changes on that front, yeah?"

He nodded, "You got it Damon. In the meantime, maybe try something new and stay out of trouble? For once?"

I smirked, "Out of... trouble? Never heard of it. Sounds complicated. Is it a repair technique?"

"For fuck's sake, Noah?"

"Yeah, yeah, I got him. Thanks for coming in, Garett. Be sure you come by so we can do something about that shitbox you're riding around in."

"It's called a cruiser, Noah."

"Depressing is what they should've called it…"

Noah walked Garrett out and I called the meeting together shortly after. Fortunately, Noah knew enough to be able to field all the questions and pitch the strategy with some assenting nods from me, and we had a plan in play for the upcoming season.

Brody, the new head honcho for Shear Performance finally reached out to schedule a meeting with me. Which surprised me, seeing that I wasn't hearing from Richard, his father. Granted we were a couple months away from the start of the racing season, so he was probably busy getting their and their clients' cars in shape just like we were. Unfortunately life doesn't stop just because we're busy.

I had never been more thankful for George, Noah and the boys. I knew that Michael would be in the office handling the paperwork, his strong suit was business while mine was the mechanics and racing. Not wanting to have anyone else tag along with me, I grabbed the keys to my '67 Mustang Fastback. I didn't want anyone worrying or asking where I was going, and if I was driving one of our cars no one would question me. All I'd have to do is tell them I wanted to see how she handled, and they'd run with it. I cranked the volume up in my radio as I drove to meet with Brody and discuss if he knew anything that had gone down that day but he was my age so who knows if he even knew.

I couldn't help but wonder why Brody was in charge; I assumed that Richard was still the force behind everything; he always seemed like a controlling prick. I slung rocks behind me as I pulled into their parking lot a bit faster than needed. I took in the lobby as I strolled into Shear Performance. It was a lot like ours, but theirs was more flashy, almost tacky... maybe I was a little bit bitter. I walked up to the receptionist, the guy was maybe a couple years younger than me, and the boredom in his face screamed that he'd rather be turning wrenches rather than be stuck doing the paperwork. I sympathized. I hated paperwork. That's why my brother Michael was helpful. He only worked 3 days a week so that he could be there to help April with Caroline, but all of our clients knew that he handled the paperwork. I dipped my chin at the young guy in front of me.

"Damon West, I have a meeting with Brody?"

His eyes lit up and he popped up out of his chair as he held his hand out for me to shake.

"Holy shit, uh, nice to meet you Damon, I'm Wyatt. Shit, sorry, I am a big fan of your racing. I had followed your dad and, well, now *your* career. I'll let Mr. Shear know you're here. Sir. Er, Mr. West." His voice trailed off.

I grinned and nodded, then handed him my card.

"Damon is fine, Wyatt. And if you ever decide, you wanna turn a wrench instead of shuffling paperwork. Let me know."

His chin dipped in acknowledgment, and he looked at the card like I'd just handed him the keys to a Ferrari. He caught himself shortly after and slowly put my card into his wallet while looking around before picking up the phone to call Brody.

While I waited, I looked out onto the garage floor to see if anything was out of the ordinary. While I scanned the garage I noticed an older Italian looking guy, with slicked back, salt

& pepper hair staring at me through the window.

I was about to go into the garage to talk to the man who was staring at me. Then Wyatt told me that Brody was ready and ushered me to his door. He knocked on the door before opening it and introducing me.

"Damon! What are you doing here, coming to check out the competition?" Brody's voice boomed as he made strides toward me. I made my way towards his desk, meeting him halfway.

"You wish, haha. How have you been, man? It's been awhile. What're you doing in the driver's seat?" I shook his hand.

"Oh, you know, I can't complain. Nobody'd listen! Mom basically put his balls in a vice. It was time for him to step down, or at least start stepping down. Though, frankly, since he loves this place more than he loves me, it probably means he'll never fully trust me to run his baby." He shrugged, returning to his desk. I nodded, understanding how much his dad cared about this garage. There was a nickname for Richard at the drag strip; it was "Ragin' Dick" especially when things didn't go his way. I never started fights but I also never backed down from a fight. Usually.

"Look man I'm not gonna beat around the bush. I got some photos from Greg, and the postage says they came from your shop. So, I wanted to know if you knew anything about them."

Confusion washed over his face and his eyebrows knitted together as he placed his hands on the desk. "Photos? Of... what? I mean, I'd be happy to look at them, though I'm not sure why anything would've come from us. Especially from us through Greg to you."

"I'd be just as confused, but I have a good reason to ask."

I passed him the envelope and he took them out and shuffled

through them.

"They're pretty old. Heh, looks like a spy took them, but hey I see a younger you." He looked up at me with a grin on his face, and I nodded in response, ruffling my hair in slight agitation.

"Yeah, well, ten years is a good amount of time. These came from the day of my dad's crash."

He blanched and looked back through slowly, studying them more carefully this time.

"Are you absolutely sure it's that day?" he asked, eyeing me.

Twenty-Eight

Jenna

It was just coffee. Right? Nothing wrong with getting coffee with a friend.

Right?

That's what I thought, at least.

"You agreed to *what*?!" exclaimed Emma.

"I'm getting coffee with Daniel. It's just coffee, Ems! Look, I just wanna see what he knows about Archer and Carly." I sighed as I pulled into the drive-thru of The Dairy Godmother.

"It's not like getting coffee with someone means you're marrying them the next day!"

"He's just so… Ugh, what's the word I'm looking for…OH! Catastrophically boring! That's the one."

I rolled my eyes while Emma laughed at herself. The speakers sprang to life with a short burst of static. I placed my order as I looked in my rearview mirror, and noticed a shiny black Mustang pull up behind me, though it wasn't the car that really caught my attention, it was the driver. The tattooed hand faded into a tattoo covered arm that was covered by a pristine white t-shirt. The tattoos looked like they'd sprang from under his shirt crawling onto his neck giving away to his chiseled jawline, his shiny aviators were a contrast. My breath hitched as the speaker hissed back at me.

"Please pull forward."

I wanted to drive so far away, so fast. I wanted to run.

What was he doing here? Fuck, and behind me, no less.

My heart was in my throat as I pulled forward, distancing myself from him. I paid for my meal and silently prayed they would *hurry*. At the speed of light, I grabbed my food and sped out of the drive-thru, praying he hadn't noticed me the way I'd noticed him. I *knew* I shouldn't be reacting this way. Like *he* had hurt *me*. Like he was the one who broke my heart. He had never done anything to hurt me. It was all of the circumstances surrounding us that seemed to be our downfall. I heard a whistling coming out of my car's speakers that snapped me back to the moment.

"Helloooo, earth to Jenna, you okay?" Emma's voice filled my car.

Shit, I forgot she was on the phone.

"Yeah. Sorry, yeah I'm okay. Well, you'll never guess who ended up behind me at Dairy Godmother." I nervously drummed my fingers on the steering wheel.

"Well, as small as Lancaster is. It could have been just about anyone. But if you say Archer, just know I will be the first one there and he may not be alive anymore by the time I'm done with him. Also, I'll get off because I have a great lawyer." Her voice shook with anger as things clattered in the background. I couldn't help but chuckle.

"I don't doubt that Ems, but thankfully homicide is not going to be needed. Plus, I don't need you ending up as a true crime documentary." I paused, hesitating to tell my best friend that I ran away from the only man I have felt strongly towards in a long time.

"It was no one. I was mistaken, I thought I saw someone we knew." I lied. I *had never* lied to her in all the years we'd known each other. We always told each other the truth and it was a tough pill to swallow sometimes but we always made it through.

"Uh, ok, weirdo. Way to make a girl have an anxiety attack over nothing."

"I'm sorry, I got a bit distracted. I swear the brain fog is real after what happened."

Why did I just lie to her? I had nothing to hide. Or did I?

As adults, Damon and I had only known each other about two months. We got along great, when we did and if he was actually willing to talk to me, but between my dad, the bar... I couldn't really tell up from down anymore. I barely remembered pulling into my driveway. Emma had filled me in on what new thing Ricky was doing or one of her cases. To be completely honest, I wasn't paying too much attention to what she was saying.

My thoughts drifted back to Damon. The way he looked, the way his fingers flexed gripping the steering wheel. The way they had felt on my skin and deep inside me. I felt a rush of heat through my body and squeezed my thighs together, seeking any relief I could from these thoughts overwhelming me. I shut my car off, grabbed Osita and got us into the house as fast as my trembling legs could carry us.

I dropped Osita off into her room, my keys and my cheeseburger on the counter and headed to my room. I closed my door, sliding out of my pants and underwear in the same motion. I lay on my bed, the cool air of my room kissing my thighs and sending a shiver through my spine. I picked up my phone, scrolling to find a photo, video, something to guide me and help ease the ache in my core.

The only picture I had of him was in my contacts.

Fuck, it'll have to do...

I focused on the memories of him, thoughts of him pinning me to the wall the only night we had fully spent together. His hot breath trailing over my neck and chest, his lips on my breasts, the way his hand felt around my throat. I dropped my phone next to me, allowing my hands to follow my imagination. My fingers traced electric trails over my body, my own hand wrapping around my throat, squeezing my breast, teasing my body. My desperate wish that it was his hands and fingers, his mouth, that it was *him* doing these things and filling me remained unfulfilled as my fingers glided through my wet folds. Brushed against my sensitive clit. Pants and moans tumbled from my mouth, and eventually so did his name as I squirmed and chased my release. I hated myself for getting myself off to the thought of him, but why?

Twenty-Nine

Damon

I realized the car in front of me was Jenna.

Fuck, now she's going to think I'm following her...

I had been trying to not think about her too much. Who was I kidding? She was all I thought about. Well, besides finding the person who sabotaged my dad, and ultimately killed him. I realized more and more that I was missing Jenna.

I pulled away from the window after getting my order to find a place to eat my burger. I was about to take my first bite when my phone vibrated in my cup holder. I rolled my eyes, set down my sandwich and picked it up, thinking my absence was finally noticed at the shop. Jenna's name flashed on my screen. I hesitated for a moment before deciding to answer the phone.

Fuck me... she does think I'm stalking her.

I bit the bullet and pressed the phone to my ear as I answered, "Hey Jenna."

She didn't say anything, instead, the melodic sound of her soft pants and whimpers greeted me instead. I licked my lips, remembering the taste of her sweet pussy. The way her skin felt, the softness of her, how wet she was for me, all of her came flooding into my mind and my cock was already rock hard just listening to her.

Shit, I shouldn't be listening to her. I shouldn't be doing this.

She clearly was over me, or so I had thought. I needed to hang up, was about to hang up, until my name escaped her. It was soft, but she repeated it, over and over again, like a prayer. I sat in the parking lot of the Dairy Godmother palming my erection, adjusting myself.

God, why did she sound even better than I remembered?

Before I could even comprehend, I heard her breath catch as she yelled my name out, signaling her climax. Quickly, I hung up, not wanting her to feel any type of way or force her to talk to me.

I sat my phone down and drove straight home instead of back to the shop. Once home, I damn near sprinted up the stairs to the shower. I didn't bother shutting the door as I turned the temperature dials, and shedding all of my restrictive clothes. My cock sprang free as soon as I'd got my jeans unbuttoned and unzipped, throbbing for attention. For *her* attention. I stepped into the water, letting it wash over me as I stroked my cock hard and rough. I remembered her fingers tracing my tattoos, her nails digging into my back, and the way she pulled my hair while she came on my tongue. The soft flesh of her thigh was such a delight to sink my teeth into. The way her cheeks flushed pink, as pants, moans and the delectable string of curse words that flowed effortlessly from her lips. Her breath hitching and the moan of pleasure as I slowly filled her, each of my piercings bringing a new gasp. The way she came as I coaxed her to stare into my eyes as she did so. I lathered up with soap as I stroked, my cock painfully hard. I panted, my need for release growing with every second.

God, I was not worthy a minute of her time. So once I got this out of my system, I was going to put all thoughts of *us* behind me and allow her to move on.

"Jenna, fuck, Kitten, I'm coming…" I repeated to myself as I gave my cock a last hard tug and came, finally watching us swirl down the drain.

There was no room for me in her life. She was a good girl, while I was just some asshole who had anger issues and was ready to fight everyone at the drop of a hat.

My erection finally subsided as I stepped out of the shower and grabbed my towel. I dried off and was just pulling on a set of sweats when there was a knock at my door.

Now just who the fuck could that be?

I walked down the stairs towards the front of the house, calling out, "I swear to fucking god, I will call the police if that's you, Nikki."

I threw open the door and there stood the same salt and pepper haired mechanic from Shear Performance, wringing his hands anxiously. I was so confused and surprised that I didn't even have the sense to ask him what he was doing here, which must have been obvious because he broke the tense silence first.

"Damon, you don't know me, but I got information about the day of your father's death." He said solemnly but shakily.

I invited him in instantly and brought him to the kitchen.

"Can I get you a drink? Water? Beer? Something stronger?"

He stared at me, fidgeting in his seat. I fought the urge to wring his neck and get him to just talk. Whatever information he had or thought he had, he felt it was important enough to show up and tell me face to face and dangerous enough to be this nervous about telling me. I could respect that. I had to respect that.

Finally, he gripped the counter to steady himself, his knuckles turning white. "Ah water for me. Please. I've ah- I've actually been in AA for the past five years, because hooch will lead to other, worse, things. That's actually what started all this."

I took two bottles from the fridge and handed him one, then took a seat on the opposite side of the island from him.

He sat there, staring at the water like it might try to bite him if he moved too quickly. In a voice just barely above a whisper, he said, "I'm sorry. I didn't really plan this out. I'm not even sure where to start with all of this."

"Well then, start from the beginning." I offered.

He nodded, took a deep breath, cracked the seal on the water, and took a gulp of it, as if God himself blessed the water and it would save all those who had been damned. I knew all too well how it felt to have my back against the wall like that, which is why at seventeen I began to fight anyone and anything in my path.

"I don't really know where the beginning is." He confessed sheepishly.

In an attempt to steel and calm myself, I threaded my hands into my hair, closing my eyes. Jenna's face filled my mind.

So much for getting her out of my system.

She seemed to calm the storm raging in me. I opened my eyes again, slowly, and took in the man sitting in front of me. I sighed and grinned at him.

"I don't even know your name, man. Maybe we can start there?" As I waited, I drank some of my own water to give me something to focus on.

He took one more deep, cleansing breath, and went ahead.

"Alright, sure. My name is Reuben. I have worked for Mr. Shear for 30 years. Back when I first started, I got myself into trouble with gambling, and the only way out I saw at the time was trusting Dick." His jaw tensed in anger at the memory.

"I get it, Dick can be a bit much." I nodded my understanding.

He shook his head. "No, with all due respect kid, you don't get it. There is no way you *could* fucking get it. He is worse, *far* worse, than anyone could ever imagine." His calloused hands fiddled with the label on his bottle clearly conflicted. I saw the pain and confusion play on his features, and when he finally made eye contact with me again, there was anger mixed with yet another emotion, resolve.

"If I tell you all this, Damon, there'll be no going back. Not for me, and not for any of the old timers over there. Not only will you finally have the truth, but I will be in big fuckin' trouble with the law. Well, that ain't nothing new, but I may be in trouble with others," he coughed into his sleeve before continuing "Dammit, but my days are almost up and I don't want to die and not make peace with my demons."

I leaned back into my seat at the island, bracing myself for whatever he was going to throw at me.

And just how the fuck would I know if he was telling the truth or not.

I took a drink of my water, wanting to appear cool and collected even though my mind was racing as fast as it ever did on a race day.

"Listen, before you tell me anything, especially if this is as bad as you're making it out to be," I paused, looking at him with a raised eyebrow before setting my bottle on the counter and continuing, "I can't promise to keep you safe. I have a friend who's a sheriff and he'll keep you as protected as he can until we figure out... all of this." It wasn't very reassuring, even to my ears. Fuck it, I know engines, racing, and rage. If he wanted emotional support and a shoulder to cry on while shedding his woes, he came to the wrong place. Hell, the first and only time I have ever fought or tried to protect someone else was that night to protect Jenna from that creep.

Oh Jenna, my sweet girl. I shouldn't have gotten so caught up in my own shit and left you alone like that. God, I'm a fucking idiot.

He relaxed, but only slightly. He was still peeling the label of the water bottle.

"I'm giving a lot less of a shit about safety these days, kid, this fucking cancer's seen to that. When you're staring down the barrel of your own mortality in a very real way, your mind gets to thinking about what you did, how things should have played out, what regrets you have... Your dad's accident was just supposed to take his car out of commission. His car. Not take him out with it." He looked directly into my eyes, his own bloodshot and glassy as if he was going to break down any minute.

I nodded for him to continue.

"I was addicted to drugs. It didn't matter what, if it got me high I chased that shit down, and Dick quickly found out if he kept me high, I would do his bidding. It's not an excuse, it's just reality. Please know this goes higher than Dick. Anyways, he gave me a job, kept me in junk, and I did his dirty work. Soon, he switched me from the shit I was on to a drug that was an anesthetic for animals. It gave me my high, and I didn't need to spend any extra. Plus, if Dick ever caught me on something else, either he himself or someone else would beat me but good. In exchange for the steady supply, money and my continued existence, I would help him and his partner. He never named him, just called him 'T.'

He took another sip of water before going back to twisting the label into a little string.

"It was my job in their little arrangement to transport the drugs, so neither of them got their hands dirty. I think you yourself have seen what 'T' can and still is doing. I heard through the grapevine about that old mule Donovan, that his oldest daughter was drugged recently. I don't think that was a coincidence."

I clenched my fist so hard I heard my knuckles cracking. The flames in hell couldn't burn hotter than the fury that I felt coursing through me. I saw Reuben's eyes go wide and I reigned myself before I did something I'd regret. I needed answers, like it or not I needed to calm down. I held up my hand placatingly.

"How did you hear about that?" I asked, watching him carefully to make sure he wasn't lying. One thing I'd picked up in my downward spiral was being able to tell when someone was blatantly lying to me.

"I forgot you had a thing for her." He chuckled darkly. "You'd always liked her and felt protective of her. Well, I hate to break it to you, kid, but you're not the only one who's got her in his sights. We're all getting older, so everyone has their kids taking over for them. T included. She wasn't going for anyone's gentle advances; so they decided to take it into their own hands." This time when he looked me in the eyes, and he wasn't backing down or shrinking away from the situation.

He was ready to face whatever consequences there might be.

I nodded, accepting what he'd told me. I knew there was no point in arguing with him right now.

"Why are you coming forward with this now? Why not at *any* fucking point in the last ten years?"

I stood and paced in front of the fridge, waiting for him to answer. It didn't make any sense to me. Why or how one could wait ten years to make things right? Ten years after the event that completely unraveled me, my family. That he was on drugs made sense for him to do it in the first place, but why wait this fucking long? Why was it when I decided to look into the wreck, when I'd found something so good, something that my mom and dad had? Why had I gotten so wrapped up in my own shit? The questions filled my head and made me feel like I was drowning. Why, just fucking why? I wanted to scream into the void, but I *needed* to calm the fuck down and get myself in check here.

"Kid, I know I should've stepped up sooner. I got a lot of fuckin' regrets and believe me that's one of 'em. I know I'm no hero, I don't think I could ever be a hero after all I had the bad shit I did. I also won't lie to you. I'm sick, Damon. I know that doesn't mean anything to you but I just want to do better by my family before I kick the bucket, more than that I have seen how your family treats their employees. They have never been just workers to you guys." His misty eyes wavered slightly as they held mine.

I knew that feeling. I recognized it, I knew what it was like to not feel that I was good enough for human kindness, for empathy or compassion. Something that was instilled in my brother and I by our father, and his father before him, was that everyone deserved to be treated with the utmost respect.

I nodded, then stepped forward and leaned on my fists on the counter..

"Listen, Reuben, you haven't done anything to me. You made a mistake trusting Dick, but guess what, we're all human. We make mistakes. It's what we do. The biggest thing is we learn from our mistakes." I leaned across the island and clapped his shoulder in solidarity. For the first time he gave me a meek smile.

I smiled back at him. "It's never too late to turn things around but that means we'll have to catch Dick in action. You think you could help me with that?" He didn't say anything, he simply nodded. There wasn't much he could say. So I decided to take it into my own hands.

"Tell you what Reuben, it's late. Why don't you leave me a way to get a hold of you, then get on home to your family, and in the morning, we'll get to work on taking that cocksucker down for what he did to all of us. What do you say?"

"I say that works for me, thank you Damon. For what it's worth, and I know it ain't worth shit, I am so fucking sorry for the part I played in all this. There's no excuse that would ever make up for it, but I am trying, truly, to make it right. Well, as right as it can be made."

Thirty

Jenna

The Wild Thyme Cafe smelled of freshly ground coffee, pastries, pies, and all the food a diner in America could offer. All of it danced into my nostrils as the bright chorus of the chimes on the door played in my ears.

"Have a seat anywhere you'd like, sugar!" A pretty waitress called out to me over a shoulder full of food bound for a waiting family.

I'd arrived a bit earlier than Daniel, partly out of habit, but partly to make sure that I picked a space I felt safe in. I chose and slid into a booth by the window, facing the door, and waited for him to arrive so we could discuss the Archer issue. About 10 minutes before the time we'd agreed on, he walked through the door to the sound of those same cheerful chimes. The same waitress who greeted me sauntered over. Her cuteness, bright eyes, and brilliant smile faltered as she saw my company.She was cute, with bright eyes and a brilliant smile, but her step and smile faltered as she saw who I was sitting with. Opening: Daniel barely glanced at her before rattling off his order as she opened her mouth to greet us. She opened her mouth to greet us, but Daniel barely glanced at her before rattling off his order. She blinked and nodded, before turning to look at me.

"And hello sweetie, I'm Veronica, what can I get *you* hun?" She asked. I noticed an accent but I couldn't place it, somewhere south I guessed.

I smiled up at her gratefully and gave my order, "I'll have the Humpty Dumpty Plate, sunny side up, and a coffee, please." She was so sweet, acting like she didn't notice that the man in front of me was not very polite.

She nodded as she jotted down both of our orders.

This had just fully convinced me that Daniel and I never would have worked, not that I'd seriously considered him much before. I could never be with someone who didn't even have the *decency* to be respectful to a waitress when ordering their food.

Now someone who fingered me under the table while he ordered dessert... GIRL get your mind out of the gutter!

"Alright, let me go put those in for you and we'll have 'em ready for y'all right away!"

"Try not to screw them up, if you can manage it." Daniel grumbled to her retreating back.

I wanted to roll my eyes at him, but suppressed the urge. Unprompted, he started rambling on about Amara's recent trip and how Archer was so proud of her. The problem with all of that for me was that he knew that I knew about the affair. His phone started buzzing on the table. He checked before turning it back over with an annoyed huff. A moment it buzzed again.

Before I could stop the question from falling from my lips, it was out there, "Are you sure you can be here? Seems like you're a pretty popular guy. I don't want to interrupt your day."

He grimaced, but then extended his hand across the table, almost in search of my hand. I nearly took it out of politeness and instinct, but then I felt his foot slide against my ankle and calf, tapping them like we were in highschool. I shifted uncomfortably in my seat, and he pulled his arm back across the table.

"Trust me Jenna, there is *nowhere* else I'd rather be." His mouth turned up in a weasel-like smile. I quickly excused myself to the ladies' room. In my rush, I almost knocked over our waitress.

"I am so sorry. I should have been looking where I was going." I apologized breathlessly.

"It's okay, darlin', but where's the fire? You rushed out of your seat like a bat outta hell! There must be a big emergency."

I let out a strangled laugh. "No, no, nothing bad. I just... just need to use the restroom."

I didn't want to raise any alarms with her, but I definitely needed to separate myself from Daniel. I had to be paranoid after what had happened to me. I'm sure I was overreacting, just like I had with Damon, but I felt the need to get out. With one look at her, I knew she didn't believe me; but thankfully she didn't press me. She just gave me a comforting smile.

"If you say so, darlin'."

I exhaled slowly, nodding as I headed toward the restroom. Behind me, I closed and locked the door. I pressed my back against the door, hoping the coolness would calm my anxiety and slow my breathing. It didn't, so I tried inhaling slowly, counting.

one...

two...

three...

four...

Keeping the same count for holding my breath and exhaling. Soon, I was able to stop the worst of the shaking. I washed and dried my hands, double checked myself in the mirror, and finally headed out the door. It couldn't have been more than five minutes, hopefully. Our server was standing in the bay by the kitchen and I went to move quietly past her, but a soft whistle had me jerking my head towards it. Veronica, our waitress, was waving me over, just out of sight of Daniel and the rest of the dining room. I started walking cautiously towards her, lifting my eyebrow in confusion. Once I reached her, she pulled me into the kitchen.

"Oh, sugar, I am *so* glad I caught you before you sat back down with *him*." She breathed a sigh of relief.

"Um, I just got out of the bathroom. What's going on, is everything ok?" I asked, pulling my lip between my teeth.

She rested her hand on my upper arm reassuringly. I could tell whatever she had to say was not going to be good. She gently squeezed my arm.

"Hon, that man you're out there with, it ain't my business, but he is a bad apple. I saw him in here before with other folks and while you were in the powder room, he took a call. Now, I didn't hear everythin', but I heard enough. Enough to know that if you go back out there, you could be in some serious trouble." Her eyes held mine with intensity, like she was trying to convey just how serious she was with a look.

I winced, lowering my head in frustration, why was this happening? I only ever did my job well. I had never shown any interest in Daniel before. Today was the first time I actively went out of my way to see him outside work. I placed my hand on hers, as the tears pricked my eyes. "Why are you trying to help me? You don't even know me." I asked slowly, meeting her caring gaze. She gave my arm a squeeze.

"I may not know you from Adam, but honey, I will not let any man cause a woman harm if I can help it. Do you have everything you need? I'm gonna sneak you out of the kitchen." I nodded and let her lead me through the kitchen to the back entrance.

"Thank you, Veronica!"

"Don't worry about it, honey, you just go home and be safe. I wouldn't let that man take you out for a second date if I were you, matter of fact, I'd just try to avoid him if you can!"

I made it to my car and started the drive home, unsure of where else to go that I would feel safe.

* * *

When I pulled up to my house, my dad was sitting outside my door. I sighed as I got out of my car and shut it. As if learning that not only one but both of my bosses weren't good men in one day, that I could have been in danger had I stuck around at my coffee date wasn't bad enough, the one person that I wanted to run to, the man that I wanted to trust and hold and comfort me I couldn't because I know he wouldn't just forgive me for thinking he was the monster who did this to me.

Instead, I had to also deal with my drunk of a father. I slumped, feeling drained and defeated.

My footsteps sounded heavy on the pavement, causing my dad to peek his head up. I expected them bloodshot and puffy, since it was a day ending in Y, but his eyes were clear. They were clear and bright for the first time in ages, but that didn't matter. The damage had already been done, and knowing him, it would be done again.

At seventeen, I'd had to help my mother make ends meet just so we wouldn't lose the house while he busied himself with drinking any extra money we had away. He had never spoken to any of us about what caused him to crawl into that bottle, but to me, at this point, it didn't matter.

He was the one man I was supposed to be able to count on, the one who was supposed to set the bar *so high* that I didn't constantly date the losers I did. The ones who lied, who cheated, and who stole from me more times than I wanted to admit. He made me do too much labor. I had to be my mother's therapist through it all, while also helping her to raise my youngest sister. To say I resented them both was an understatement. I stopped in front of him.

"Gemmy." His smile lit up, but his voice shook with concern, sensing my mood; he hadn't used that nickname since I was eight years old. He stood up slowly, the drinking and years of hating himself clearly took its toll on his body. The once boisterous, large man who used to pick me and Kris up with ease was gone. In spite of everything, I felt a pang of guilt shoot through my chest for just a moment.

But only for a moment.

"What are you doing here, *Dad?*" I asked, unlocking my door to allow us access to my house; I really didn't want to become known as *that* neighbor.

"That's a fair question, Gems, I-" I held my hand up to stop him, and ushered us into my house. A house that he had never seen until now. He stopped just short of the hall threshold, staring at the same old racing photo that caught Damon's attention that one night. I watched him as his fingers brushed the photo.

"Oh, Miles, I sure made a mess of things this time, didn't I?" His voice was so soft I almost didn't hear him. He turned to me and his misty eyes met mine. I motioned him to continue following me. When we were around the corner from Osita, she chirped her greeting at us. My dad tilted his head in confusion as I went to her room to get her out of her sleeping hammock. Dad's face was full of surprise as I passed him with her in tow.

"Come on, follow me to the kitchen, Dad. We can discuss why you're here while I feed this little princess." I lifted her so that we were face to face and kissed her nose gently. The man who helped give me life chuckled as he followed. I heard a phone start to buzz and turned to see my dad rejecting the call and putting his phone back in his pocket.

"Who was that?" I asked, fighting the flashback to Daniel this morning.

"No one as important as you, Gemmy. He can wait." He pointed at Osita with a grin, "I can't believe you'd let a wild animal in your home like it's some kind of pet." he chided, somewhere between amused and horrified.

I resisted the urge to roll my eyes.

"Because of her injury, she'll likely never be able to be released into the wild. She's been around humans since she was a baby, well, an even smaller baby." I set her down as I blended some berries, milk and some crickets, since she still couldn't chew yet. My dad sat down, watching her suspiciously. "I promise she won't bite you. As long as you're nice to her. I'm sure Kristen told you that."

He nodded and tentatively, very gently, offered her a finger to sniff. "She did. We haven't talked much but when we were catching up, she definitely told me about your little friend here. She told me about her and Mark, Damon told me about you all. I was-"

"Dad, what the hell are you doing here?" I interrupted the beginning of his ramble. He took his finger away from Osita, who turned her attention back to her shake.

He lowered his eyes to the floor, either searching for an answer or in shame I didn't know which. Finally, he found his words.

"Gem, I want to apologize. I am so, so sorry I was such a shitty father. I let survivors' guilt and grief get in the way and I missed out on the past ten years of your and Kristen's life," he stated as he slid into a dining chair. I sat her protein shake down and looked at him. I studied him for a moment.

"Excuse me?" my eyebrow arched. He raised his eyes to find mine before he answered.

"I said, I am sorry Jenna. I'm fully ready to accept it if you don't want to forgive me. I don't think I deserve your forgiveness, any of you, your mother and sister, too. I screwed up, deeply. Maybe to the point that it can't be fixed, but I am ready to explain to everyone what happened, to make amends and take the spot I should never have left vacant. I just hope you'll hear me out." He said, maintaining eye contact with me, his mouth in a straight line. Just looking at him up close, I could tell he was tired of carrying the baggage around for the past ten years. When I placed my hand atop the hand that had been so sure and steady, it was warm and now trembled.

I shook my head slightly. It wasn't that I was against forgiving him, but this wasn't the first time he wanted to be forgiven. It was, however, the first time he was sober when he asked for it. I squeezed his hand slightly.

"Dad, I can see that you are finally sober and making an effort. How many times have we been down this road, though? I *want* to believe that you will stay sober, I really do… but it's only been a few weeks. I am so proud of that effort you've put in but right now I just… I can't," My voice was shaky and my eyes started to burn with the pricking of tears. I wanted nothing more than to hug him and sob into his shirt about the ten years of awful exes, the stress of putting myself through college. To celebrate the fact that I graduated at the top of my veterinary tech classes and discuss all the stuff he had missed out on. Instead, here we both were, on the verge of tears. "At least not right now, but if you keep the effort up, I'd be willing to discuss this later."

His other hand slid over mine and squeezed it, though he tried to hide the disappointment that flickered across his face.

"I completely understand, Gemmy." His voice was soft, fragile. Trying to ease the tension that hung like humidity in the air, I offered a small smile.

"How about I make us some coffee and we can talk about whatever you want, maybe we could talk about cars?" I straightened up to check on Osita, who was desperately trying to get in the blender. My dad and I both laughed.

"She reminds me of you as a baby. You never appreciated it when your mother and I didn't feed you when you wanted," he said as I made my way over to blend her food and pour it into her dish.

"What can I say, we're strong young women who know what

we want, aren't we Osita?" She chattered happily as I pressed the button on the coffeemaker.

Over the next couple of hours, dad and I sipped coffee and chatted about cars, Osita, my job, and the unexpected death of Damon's father. I'd stopped going to the racetrack when I was thirteen, since I wanted to spend my time volunteering at the animal shelter or at the mall with my friends. I had never realized before now just how connected my current life was with my past.

Thirty-One

Damon

I had called Don after Reuben left last night to see if he'd be willing to meet me at the shop, but the call had gone to voicemail, and every time I called after it seemed like his phone was shut off. That made me worried, but the only thing I could do about it was hope that he wasn't crawling back into the bottle for some reason. I tried to be positive, like maybe he was with his wife making up for lost time, or with Kristen helping her and her fiance plan their wedding.

Or maybe he was with Jenna, since he'd been so worried about her after the incident.

I didn't blame him. I wanted to drop everything on my plate and run to her, hold her in my arms until she knew she was safe. Until she never questioned that safety again. Until she knew that I would *never* intentionally hurt her.

Unless it was in the bedroom.

The Lord knows I couldn't deny that woman a damn thing

if she asked, it'd be like denying the sun to shine.

Finding that my father had been murdered, unintentionally or not, was a hell of a tailspin. We all grew up with racing. We had all known that accidents could happen, but to have someone step up and admit that they had sabotaged his car? That was just insane.

The drive to the shop was easy, and my mind was distracted with turning over all the new information I'd learned, trying to fit it into the bigger picture.

There was still so much I couldn't totally wrap my head around, like why sabotage my dad's car at all.

The races were a big deal for our town, and especially our shops, but sabotaging the competition like that?

It didn't add up.

When I pulled into the lot at the shop, I saw that a few of the other guys were already there, and Don was looking at the undercarriage of someone's Mustang, sipping a greasy styrofoam cup of coffee. After nodding a greeting to Liam and Noah, I stepped into my office to take some notes on what Reuben had said, and I called Don in to join me. I wanted to get whatever dirt he had on Richard to see if it could help us devise a plan. He came in and he seemed much happier since we'd staged our little intervention; I knew he was going to AA and had a therapist to help him. It seemed to be working wonders.

I just hoped Jenna would give him a chance.

I know I was biased since my dad was dead and, really, I can't imagine the hell that his girls went through, but I still felt that Don deserved a second chance. At least, if he could really keep the bottle away for good this time. For the first time since reconnecting with Jenna as adults, I realized that

145

both of us were fucked up in our own way.

Don walked into my smaller office in the shop with two cups of coffee, and I smiled at him.

Maybe when everything had settled down I could try my shot with Jenna again. I missed her, the scent of her hair, how she felt in my arms and hands, the way she tasted, the way she moaned my name.

Shit.

I needed to cut *those* thoughts of her in front of her father.

"Hey Damon, what's goin' on?" He asked jovially, setting my coffee in front of me before seating himself in the chair across from my desk.

"A lot actually, want to talk to you about some things, but what the hell's got you in such a chipper mood this morning?"

"I saw Gemmy last night. We had a nice long talk, about cars, the race track, her work, hell even that little racoon puppy she's got over there."

"Kit, and her name is Osita." I couldn't stop myself from correcting him.

He snapped his fingers in response, "That's the one! Damon, I just don't understand why you two kids can't work this out, she is *also* hurting. Hell, I mean, I was a drunk for ten years and my wife stuck by my side. I don't get it, I mean, I heard stories of how you went through ladies without batting an eyelash, but Noah hasn't complained about you with a girl or beating anyone up since I joined your team." He let out a chuckle as he set down his coffee. I tried to mask the hurt with a smile.

"What can I say, I'd love nothing more, Don, but we both heard Jenna. I'm just trying to respect her wishes. Maybe once everything settles down, we can talk about it, but until then I am resigned to my suffering. You already know that no other woman even comes close to her."

He nodded, and I reached for my coffee, taking a sip. "I don't suppose you know anything about a kid working for Shear named Wyatt, would you?"

His eyebrows furrowed, and then he raised an eyebrow at me. "I mean I don't *personally* know him but I *have* heard through the grapevine that he's a good kid. Though I'm willing to bet that's not really why you're asking me about him, is it?"

I smirked, "No, it's not."

* * *

I should have known he probably wouldn't know much. That was okay because he wanted to talk to me about Jenna and how she was doing. It stung me, but I also wanted to know that she was okay.

Aside from that phone call with her needy pants and moans, but she sounded just fine then. Get your fucking mind right, West, her dad is still sitting right there.

I took a gulp of my coffee to make sure my thoughts were well masked. Or that I didn't say them out loud.

"I'm just sayin' Damon, I like you kid, hell, I always have. You got a good thing going here, and I want you two to succeed. From everything I heard, you made her happy, and you've been like a lovesick puppy so-"

"Hooey, kids these days, well they wouldn't know what true love or true commitment meant if it jumped up and bit them right on the tuchus!" George interrupted with a laugh from the doorway with Noah, Liam, and Jax trailing him. All of the guys that were my age just all laughed at the two older men and rolled their eyes. Noah had something in his eye that he removed with his middle finger, but I'm sure that was unrelated.

"Since when did this become a team meeting? I don't remember asking you all in here and I damn sure didn't tell you to slack on your jobs. Our clients expect us to have their vehicles done in a timely manner, *and* we are *quickly* running out of time before the start of race season."

George let out another laugh, "Hogwash, son. You're not worried. We have yet to not get things done when they need doin', and I know I don't plan on startin' now. We're here to help you with whatever it is ya need help with." and sat down slapping Don on the shoulder.

The guys that were closer to my age crowded in, making noises of agreeing with what George said. I rubbed my forehead in frustration.

"Fine. We know who messed with my dad's car. He was drugged up and forced to do it, so I want to go after the real bastard who did it. If anyone wants to be left *out* of the plan I completely understand because this might get you into more trouble than it's worth. You guys are my family as much as Michael, his wife, Caroline and Mom. I won't think less of any of you for sitting this one out."

They all looked at me as if I had suggested that they never touch a wrench again in their life. The silence was thick in the air, uncomfortable. All I wanted to do was get out of there, I was also trying to step out of my comfort zone. They were family and yeah, sure, you fight sometimes with family but you can lean on them too. I wasn't a great person, I had no illusions about that. I'd put my mom through hell which she didn't need after dad passed. She never blamed me but it was my fault, *only* my fault. Just because I was lost didn't mean that I needed to act out.

The courts, also, could have not taken pity on the kid whose dad passed. I could have been arrested and stuck in jail for any number of things: street racing, fighting, underage drinking and more. I was lucky, luckier still that I was surrounded by people who never gave up on me. I remember when a few kids I went to highschool with were taking some type of drug they called Tranq that acted like a roofie. It wasn't for humans but animals. Something about that just clicked into place for me.

George's hand landed on my head, "Well, you got us here now kid, and I don't think anyone's leaving. Whatcha thinking about so hard?"

I scratched the stubble on my chin and glanced back to Don before answering, "Didn't you say the man that attacked Jenna worked with her?" I could see the gears turning in his head as he took a sip of his coffee.

"That's what Jenna said when I gave her the name. Why? Do you think she's connected to something?" He said brusqucly as he made to stand up.

"*No*, not at all," I shook my head for emphasis and held a hand out placatingly.

I stood from my desk and moved to the door of my office and shut it firmly, ensuring that nothing left the room and ruined my plan.

"Alright, if you're all in on this," I made eye contact with everyone including Don who looked like he was ready to rip my head off for even bringing Jenna up.

Noah, Liam, and Jax looked like I was about to just drop something about the race season. George was the last one I made eye contact with and his face just said 'I am too old for this shit.' I couldn't blame him. I should have let things go, but I wanted this to be fully behind me when I made Jenna mine.

There I go again thinking she would even want me. What the hell was wrong with me? I promised to put her behind me so she can move on to someone who deserves her. "We've got two connects with the fuckers who killed my dad. One at least for sure, that's the one I was just talking about, and the other is a kid named Wyatt. We know Dick's involved, and I think someone at Jenna's clinic is too."

Thirty-Two

Jenna

Kristen had dragged me out with her friends and mom to help her find her dress for the wedding. As I was scanning through the racks of white the sinking feeling in the pit of my stomach returned. I was so happy for my little sister, but why did I also feel so hollow? Was it because, due to my own stupidity, I shoved the only man who made me feel *anything* away? Was it because I was the oldest and I felt like the timeline was all messed up? My sister joined me scanning the rack, without making eye contact.

"Have you reached out to him?" she asked as she pulled a dress off the rack to examine it.

This was the last thing I wanted to talk about so I opted to play stupid hoping she'd let it go. This was supposed to be her day.

"To who?"

She huffed, even as a child she had a flair for the dramatic,

"The boogeyman? Damon, sissy. He loves you. You know.'"

I looked at her stunned; it had been maybe a month as adults that we had known each other. "What are you talking about? It hasn't been *near* enough time to know if he loves me. Besides, today is about finding the perfect dress for you. Can we please focus on *you* and not *my* issues?"

She rolled her eyes at me and slid the dress she was holding back on the rack.

"*I* would marry Mark in a trash bag in front of a judge. *I* don't need all this... mess. This is for his mother, and well ours, because those two need this," with a sigh she continued as her eyes met mine. "-and you're wrong. I remember when we were kids you two were inseparable. He hated other girls. The only one he liked was you. He was always so protective over you. He's loved you since we were kids."

How would she have known she would have been too young?

As if reading my mind, she continued, "I remember us all playing together and I've seen the photos, if he was in them with us he was always holding your hand. Time may have come and gone, and well everyone who knows him knows about how he was as a teen and well now... now he has a past, but doesn't everyone? I mean Mark sure did before he met me. It changes nothing. You two can make it past this. I promise you he'll forgive you, and he'll understand."

As if it were that simple.

* * *

Kristen called for me while she was in the dressing room. Seeing her in the white gown made my breath catch, and I watched mesmerized as the sequins danced and shimmered in the light. She looked like a princess until I made eye contact with her in the mirror, the moment was broken. She appeared as though the dress was constricting her, making her face look strained. Her eyes were brimming with tears and had a glassy appearance. I hurried towards her and embraced her tightly, then looked at her with concern.

"Kris, what's wrong? Did something happen? Should I get Mom?" She held my hands, sniffled, and wiped away her tears.

"No, I don't want to go through with this. I can't handle all the attention. Why can't Mark and I just get married the way we want?"

I hugged her once more and whispered, "Do you trust me?"

She sighed and replied, "More than anything," while returning the hug.

Pulling back with a smile, I asked her, "What dress do you envision yourself getting married in at city hall?"

She pointed to a knee-length dress made from ivory lace tulle, in an A-line design, "Definitely that one. I love how it's a classic dress without being over the top. Jenna, you know our mom and Mark's will both have a fit."

Without hesitation I waved the Bridal consultant over, handed her my credit card and told her to ring up the dress that Kristen said, but the consultant and Kristen were befuddled by my actions.

Without missing a beat I smiled and pointed to one of the dresses on the wall, "Kristen, help me in this dress then call Mark, tell him to find something nice to wear and take you to city hall in the gown you want. There is absolutely *no reason* for a bride to do something she doesn't want to do on her day," I turned to the bridal consultant.

"Do you have someone who can touch up Kristen's makeup?"

"Absolutely ma'am."

"Good, get her, and as soon as I'm in this dress, have her come in here and get my sister ready to go. Sissy, I'm getting you that dress, and you and Mark are going to run down to that courthouse. I'll deal with them, got it?"

A few moments later, I walked out in a dress that neither Kristen nor I would ever be caught dead in. It had the puffiest sleeves since the eighties, like something our mother would've worn. I was hoping, praying, that me walking out in *this* dress would cause such a shock that it would allow Kristen enough time to slip out of the shop and meet Mark outside.

So they could marry on their terms.

They never wanted all the fuss, they just wanted each other. She would have married him with a ring pop, or a ring that came out of those little fifty cent toy machines they have outside of stores. Once the bridal consultant gave me the nod, I waltzed out of the dressing room, wondering what my life would be in the next five years. Would I still be single? My mind drifted back, as it had been doing since that day in the Dairy Godmother drive-thru to that tattooed god, to thoughts of us at six or seven running through the race track with our fingers intertwined.

I was the one to leave him when we were fifteen. I had just decided that I no longer wanted to go to the racetrack; severing my attachment to Damon, my father and the other members of our racing family. It was me *again* choosing to distance myself from a man who had done nothing but, since we were kids, protect me. It was my own stubborn stupidity. I needed to be the one to win him back, he thought he was the one who was undeserving and fucked up. The one who had messed us up in some way.

I sighed, but as I got closer to my mom and Kristen's friends, I plastered a smile on my face.

If he only knew.

I stood in front of them fluffing out the bottom of the dress. The puffy sleeves were so large that they were practically covering my face. The lace bodice itched my torso. I wouldn't have been surprised if this dress actually was seriously stashed away since the 1980s.

Everyone was giggling at me when I saw my sister slipping out the front doors all dressed and ready to go. She smiled widely at me and blew me a kiss as we made eye contact and she made her way to Mark's brand new shiny black Maxima. He slid out of the driver's side, in a black button down and matching pants and shoes. He ran to open her door but she stopped to let him get a good look at her. He picked her up and twirled her around, setting her down and gently kissing her before quickly ushering her into the car. As they pulled away my mother's voice ripped my eyes from the window.

Meanwhile, I made a show of preening for our mom, Mark's, and all her friends.

"Yes, yes all good and funny, but where is Kristen, Jenna?" Mom asked, her smile slowly fading.

I made eye contact with my mom, and composed myself in front of her. She already thought that I was the disappointment in the family. She wanted me to marry my last boyfriend; claiming that my 'biological clock was running out.' I rolled my eyes internally hoping my face didn't show my emotion but according to Damon I was an open book and wore all of my expressions *very* plainly.

Unless he could just read me that well.

I pinched my arm that I had behind my back to stop thinking

about him and answer my mom.

"Well," I started with a smile. "Her and Mark are on their way to city hall right this second."

Mom's face went pale, "What do you mean she and Mark are headed to city hall, Jenna?! You better be kidding, she might be the only one to get married."

I sighed and rolled my eyes, not even trying to hide it.

"Amelia," one of the bridesmaids beckoned her to sit down.

"Listen, *mother*, I know you think of me as being the disappointment of the family. What I think you forget, or at least you want to forget, is that while you were 'helping' dad, you neglected Kris; I was seventeen, dammit, and I had to take care of a thirteen-year-old! I didn't get to do anything a normal seventeen-year-old did!" I refused to back down and let her talk down to me any longer. A bridal consultant rushed in and escorted me to the back to change and to help calm the tension in the air.

I apologized profusely to the bridal consultant. Her name tag read Scarlett.

"Please, that was more tame than most bridal parties. I've seen people throw punches," She giggled and then caught my eye in the mirror as she dragged the zipper down. "For what it's worth, I'm sorry that your mom treated you that way after you did something super thoughtful for your sister. Sometimes people let their own wants cloud over the wants or needs of others."

I smiled at her, she was so wise.

I pulled on my own clothes and snuck out to the parking lot where I noticed a black SUV parked a block away. A man was in the driver's seat, aviators covering his eyes but he was clearly staring in my direction. Shrugging it off, I continued to get into my car, and pressed send on my phone. A short three rings later my best friend was on the line.

"Hey Jen, how was dress shopping with Kristen, and the curmudgeon?"

I checked my mirrors as I pulled out onto Main, and saw the SUV maneuver onto the road, heading the same way I was.

"It was an *experience*. Also, Kristen and Mark got married today, or currently are rather." I paused and checked behind me, the black SUV was still there; a few cars behind. "Um… Ems I think I'm being followed."

"Followed? Like Damon came to his senses and pulled his head out of his ass and is now following you like a lost puppy? Because I could get behind that."

"What? God, no, Emma. Like there is a creepy ass man in a big black SUV, like some sort of thriller movie kind of followed."

"Oh shit really? In Lancaster of all places? Weird. Can you make a left turn? And then make a square to see if you're actually being followed or if you're just being paranoid."

I sighed, my knuckles turning white as I gripped the steering wheel tighter. What was my life becoming nowadays?

"I'm on it," as I turned left without signaling. "First left down. Three more to go."

"Let me know Jenna, I am texting my associate to meet you. Just in case."

Three more left turns and sure enough I was being followed.

"Well fuck. Where am I headed Emma?"

She chuckled nervously. "I don't know how you're so calm."

Thirty-Three

Damon

"Are you sure you can trust whoever it is?" Noah asked cautiously. I paced the small office that was now even smaller with everyone in there. I was just relieved Michael hadn't needed to be in the office of late. He'd be *livid* that I was digging up the past, he wanted to just forget it and move on. Which, I understood, especially since he had April and Caroline. In one of my drunken stupors, at eighteen I think, I know I was underage but I remember telling mom that it never set right with me that nothing had been wrong with the care until that last race she agreed with me. I know she didn't want to think about it anymore than she needed to. She lost her best friend and love that day.

"I honestly don't know, but I have to figure this out for myself so I can move on with my life and now knowing that there is a connection possibly to Jenna, well, that concerns me a bit." I stated plainly.

Donovan still looked as if he could strangle me, bit out. "Explain. Now."

I took a step back, into the wall unfortunately, not wanting to provoke him or poke the metaphorical bear. I could almost certainly take him, but if I ever wanted a chance with Jenna I knew that no matter their relationship she wouldn't take too kindly to me and her father brawling.

"The name you gave me stating he worked with her has the same first initial of a last name as the mysterious guy lacing and providing the drugs to people. My source, who everyone will meet when I gain a bit more of their trust, mentioned it was animal medication."

Now I may not be the smartest man out there, hell I didn't even go to college, but my time running the streets when I was younger told me that if the math was mathing the way it should be then you were on the right track. Kinda like if it looks like a duck and quacks like a duck it's a duck.

I continued piecing it together with what I had, I thought back to the night Jenna was drugged. I thought about that older man's hands on her, how he cornered her. The way he trapped her like she was an animal. I wanted to take down Richard and whoever the fuck this Mr. T. was.

The phone rang.

Shit there was no more time to talk this over with my team. I held up my hand and answered the phone which signaled to everyone that it was time to get back to work. One of our customers was asking about their car they hoped to have back before the start of the race season which was approaching soon.

I assured them that it would be finished in time, and I was probably even telling the truth. I may have been known for my temper, but my team and I were damn good at what we did. Once off the phone I headed to test another client's car on the dyno.

Hell, we'd even expanded to taking out of state customers. It was a bit surreal. Dad would have been so proud, and I mean Pops would have too. I dismissed the feeling.

When did I become so fucking sentimental?

I supposed I have always held onto sentimental things like the family garage. I loved being in my zone, and *this* was my zone. This was what I was meant to do, work with my hands.

To hold Jen-

a hand landed on my shoulder, causing me to jump slightly and knocking me out of my latest reverie. I spun around ready to fight with a wrench in my hand.

Michael threw up his hands, signaling that he was not a threat. "It's just me, man. Wow, I haven't seen you jump in a while you really were in the zone weren't you?"

I chuckled, trying to hide my nerves. I was really on edge that day and had to remind myself to pull it together.

"I guess, but hell, here I'm usually like this. There's nothing quite like hearing the engine purr and finding out what makes it tick, and when I'm listening to that engine tell her story…" Suddenly, I remembered something, "Wait, I thought you weren't going to be in until Tuesday?"

He shoved his hands into his pockets and huffed, "Can't an older brother just spend time with his younger brother without having an ulterior motive?"

Setting the wrench down I eyed him suspiciously. "You have my niece who is the cutest thing ever and you *willingly* want to be in a dirty garage with a bunch of guys?" I smirked devilishly at him, "April and you get into an argument again?"

Thirty-Four

Jenna

Once I pulled up to Emma's office, her coworker Sean, dressed in a dark blue suit and mirrored aviators of his own hopped out of his car with a pistol neatly tucked into the band of his pants, but clearly visible against his light collared shirt. The black SUV drove past without a second glance.

After watching it drive past and disappear around the corner, he opened my car door, and spoke gently as if he was speaking to a frightened child.

"Hey Jenna, I'm glad to see you again! Though I really wish it were under different circumstances. You okay?"

I nodded as he ushered me into their office, keeping his focus up and down the street, and we noticed them circle back to the front of the building just as he shut the door. He brought us into his office where they wouldn't be able to see us.

"Why are we hiding back here like we're children? Why are they following me?" The tears threatened to spill as my voice raised.

He stopped short turning toward me. " I can only speculate. I know Emma had mentioned that you've been drugged recently. Do you have any idea who did it?"

I shrugged, "I mean, I know who gave me the drugged drink, but I genuinely don't think he'd be the one to actually have the balls to do it. If that makes sense?"

He clearly didn't believe that, and shrugged noncommittally, "You'd be surprised what people you think you know are capable of."

I leaned back against the wall and felt myself shivering uncontrollably, not from the cold but the sheer uncertainty of my whole situation. I could feel myself spiraling into a panic attack, my breath coming in short bursts.

Why did Veronica help me that day? Was it some goodness in her? Is she working with them? Some good in the world?

God, was I just becoming cynical on top of everything else?

* * *

After I got myself calmed down, I called my Emma to see if I could stay with her but as soon as I heard Ricky in the background I quickly excused myself. Calling my parents wasn't something I wanted to do, but I guess desperate times call for desperate measures. My dad answered on the second ring.

"Gemmy? You never call me. Is everything okay?"

The panic in his voice was hard to miss, as was the mixture of hammer hitting metal mixed with music. I tried to feign confidence, even though right now that was the last thing I felt.

"Yeah dad I'm good. Ah, listen, we think I am being followed. I have been *encouraged* to stay with someone." I looked over at Sean who nodded gravely at me, "Do you think Osita and I could stay with you and mom for a bit?"

I wanted to throw up. This was the worst. I thought that I would never have to look back after I had walked out but Osita and I weren't safe on our own right now. I didn't want to put anyone else in danger but right now I didn't have a choice.

"Of course sweetie, you know our door is always open to you. However long we need to get this figured out, it's fine."

"You might want to check with-"

"Absolutely not, I know she'd agree with me. Hell I'm pretty sure we can convince her to let in that wild rat you've got."

"She's a raccoon kit, dad, and-"

"I know Gems, I'm just teasing you, trying to lighten the mood. Well, as much as it can be... She can stay too, behaves better than some kids I know. Tell me where you're at, and I'll be there quick as lighting."

How did it come to this?

A few minutes later, and I was following my dad and one of his co-workers, an older man, to my house, mentally making a list to grab from my house for Osita and I as we drove.

I pulled into my driveway, dad and the older man parking on the other side. My dad was the first one who hopped out and walked over to my window.

"Jenna, stay put for a moment here with George. I am going to canvas the area." Dad said as he patted my hand on the steering wheel.

The older man, George, apparently, replaced my father at the driver's side window.

"He thinks he's fuckin' Rambo or some shit," The old man

said with a wink to me, then held his hand out for what I assumed would be a hand shake.

Nope.

He gave the back of my hand a quick peck. "So you're the chick who has Damon's balls in her purse. If you ask me you're *way* too pretty for him."

I chuckled as my hand retreated to my side. I slid out of my car joining the older gentleman. "I don't think we've been properly introduced. I'm Jenna, Don's oldest daughter. I- I guess I was unaware Damon talked about me to anyone." I felt a sensation of warmth in my cheeks.

"I'm George. Don't think anything of it. I have known Damon and well, your dad for, well, since long before you and Damon were both alive. I worked with Damon's dad." He responded with an easy smile.

Dad came around the corner with a smile. "I don't see anything around here but I wouldn't put it past whoever you saw will be here at some point. You know Gem, I've been watching a *bunch* of those Action type shows with police and stuff. Have you checked your car to see if there was a tracking device?"

George and I just looked at him like he was crazy but apparently we both decided to not question him. With a shrug we looked over the car to see if there were any devices. Satisfied that there either were none, or we didn't actually know what we were looking for, we all made our way inside.

I offered the men a lemonade, and a seat on my couch, while I went to pack Osita and I's bags. I offered her to my father and much to my surprise he took her and bounced her gently like a baby. George let out a loud bellow of laughter. I grabbed her food. Dad grabbed the bag out of my hands as I got Osita in her carrier. We walked out of the house when the men gave each other a knowing look. Whatever they had up their sleeves I wasn't going to be happy about.

"Jenna, you are not going to be happy about this, but we think it would be best to take your car to the garage, and one of the guys will escort you wherever you need to go. We'll get you and Osita settled first, but we also think we need to talk to the police."

George cleared his throat. "Good news there, is that we have one we trust. If someone is out here drugging people then I am sure people are being paid off."

I wanted to fight for my freedom and to live my life the way I wanted, but right now I was just too tired to fight them.

Thirty-Five

Damon

I met Reuben at Wild Thyme Cafe, to let him in on the start of the plan. We still needed one of the most crucial components.
Wyatt.

That boy was *dying* to turn wrenches and I was going to have an opening soon. George was going to be retiring, or at least easing into it. Ethel has been breathing down all or our necks to kick him out of the garage but that would be like taking wings from a bird that could soar. Though maybe they could take that motorcycle trip across the United States. Hell they could go see George's favorite baseball team in Oklahoma. Ever since I was little I remember he would bribe my dad to figure out how to play it in the shop since baseball season was during our busiest time of year. I shoved those thoughts out of my head as I sat down across from him.

His face was anxious.

"Were you followed?" he whispered.

Shaking my head I reached for the menu.

"If anyone questions why we're together just say you're looking at buying one of my cars." I said back, quietly. He tightened his lips and nodded in response.

"Breathe, Reuben. You're no good to anyone if you go and have a heart attack on us."

The waitress sauntered over to the table and sat down two glasses of water, before being interrupted by the man who tried to drug Jenna and another man I didn't know. Her smile faltered, but she recovered quickly as she affixed her well practiced smile.

The waitress mumbled under her breath. I wasn't entirely sure what she said but it sounded a lot like "Trouble is back."

She quickly shuffled to the back, grabbing one of the cooks to come from the back with her. He was a big man, I sure as hell wouldn't want to bump into him in a dark alley. They eyed the men, and were watching as four other men came in the front door. Reuben's eyes went wide in panic and he damn near slipped below the table. I looked over my shoulder nonchalantly and realized one of the men was Richard.

None of them looked happy.

Well well well... I wonder who pissed in his cornflakes.

Reuben damn near sprinted to the bathroom, while I just acted like nothing was going on. In spite of my nonchalant attitude, the air felt like one of those cheesy mob films from the 40s, to the point I would've sworn they were going to bust out the cheesy lingo and tommy gun. I watched out of my peripheral as the waitress dropped off their menus and waters at the tables. She was trying to keep her distance when one of the men, who was unknown to me, but about the same age as Richard, grabbed her wrist, his disgusting smile evident on

167

his face. The cook started towards them. He released her but not before saying what he needed to her. She pretended that it didn't bother her, but the expression of disgust was clearly visible on her face.

"Are you alright, miss?" I asked with concern. She feigned a smile and gave a slight nod.

"Just another day as a waitress, at least they kept their hands above my waistline. What can I get for you and your friend?"

I placed my order with her. I was just about certain that Reuben had already climbed out the bathroom window.

I waited for a few moments before getting our waitress's attention and asking for my order to go instead, and a bunch of food for the shop. A little while later, I grabbed my to-go orders for the boys and myself.

It was Saturday, two weeks before the race season. Since we were all so busy, I knew they would appreciate the sandwiches for lunch. I left my bill and the tip on the table, and snuck out unnoticed, which I was thrilled about. As soon as I made it back to my car I looked up and saw Richard, another older man who I didn't know but judging by his suit he had some money, and a younger guy that I recognized as another veterinarian that Jenna worked for.

Okay so for sure whatever drug they're using in place of a date rape drug is meant for animals.

They paid no attention to me as I fiddled around my car keeping an eye on the men.

Sensing movement out of the corner of my eye, I glanced in that direction, and sure enough it was Reuben sneaking around trash cans. Thankfully the others were on the far side of the restaurant, and unaware of him clambering about. This whole situation made me want to laugh when I was transported into one of those old TV cop shows my gramps used to love so much. The problem was I wasn't a cop, hell, I don't think I could even be classified as a vigilante. I was just a guy, that was just trying to find the truth and eventually, hopefully, win back my girl. I waited until the men got in their cars and drove away a few minutes later, leaving the waitress inside looking visibly upset at what I guessed was an unpaid bill.

Reuben finally wandered over to my car. I chuckled softly as I pulled an extra sandwich from the bag.

"Shit, I'm sorry-" I held up my hand to stop him.

"Don't worry, man I get it. If they'd have seen us together it would have blown our plan all apart."

I handed him the sandwich, he just nodded and headed toward his car. My own roared to life and I guided us out of the parking lot and headed towards the garage. Michael called me on the way, and I had to turn sadly down the sound of the song 'Badland Saints' by The Dirty Hooks

"Hey. Greg keeps blowing my shit up, something about dues and paperwork being late? Do you have any idea what the fuck he's talking about?"

Paperwork and dues were Michael's job. I gripped the steering wheel harder and gritted my teeth.

"Well, Michael, that is your gig, man, so if Greg is blowing up your stuff about dues and paperwork for the season, that is something *you* should be on top of. It being vaguely fucking important for our careers." I growled.

He huffed, "No shit, Damon, I know I've got dad brain sometimes, but I am *certain* that I filled it out and sent it in, or at least I could have sworn I did. Hell, I could do all of that in my sleep. I've been doing it for years. Early too, not that you'd know."

Thirty-Six

Jenna

We pulled up to mom and dad's house, and I noticed that the yard looked cut and there were flowers in flats just waiting to be planted. I looked over at my dad, the pride evident in the swelling of his chest. He really seemed to be taking his sobriety seriously this time, and I wondered what had finally clicked for him. It was good to see him stepping up for mom.

Ugh, mom. I know she hasn't had a chance to cool down yet, I wonder how she's taking all this...

I may have hated being here, but I was glad that I had a place to hide out. I still wasn't going to go down without a fight.

Dad turned to me, "So, I was thinking about it on my drive to your house, Gems. I don't think it's a good idea for you to be going to work at the center until you have a chance to talk to Garrett."

I sighed. I should have known he wasn't going to let this go that easily. "Fine, let's go talk to him now."

"Are you sure you don't want to wait at least a day?" He gave me a sideways glance.

I smiled. "Nope, no way. I am ready to take back my life. I refuse to lay down and live in fear while whoever is doing this to me gets to dictate how. I'm done hiding." I trembled with a newfound determination, my nerves were electrified.

He wiped his hand across his face in frustration and sighed, "Fine. Also, head's up, I... well, I forgot to tell your mom you were coming so she might have a coronary," He chuckled, and reached over to pat my knee. "I am so glad to see you still have some of that spunk left in you kiddo."

This will be interesting.

We started walking towards the door, Osita sitting quietly in her carrier, taking in the new smells.

"Alright, you get our little friend here snuck into your room, and I'll run interference with mom. Speed and stealth, that'll get you in. Speed and stealth."

"Dad?"

"Yes, Gems?"

"Maybe start watching something other than action movies after this?"

"Your concerns will be noted in the after action report."

Dad opened the door and immediately sought out my mother, who fortunately had her back turned to me. For my part, I very quietly made my way to my room with Osita and my duffle bag in tow.

After I tucked her into my old bedroom, I heard dad talking to mom about what was going on before we went to speak to the sheriff. She had a look of worry and anger on her face when I entered the kitchen. She seemed unimpressed with what they had just discussed. There was no doubt in my mind that she was still angry with me for the scene I caused at the bridal store, but that doesn't change the fact that I hated being responsible for all this.

Thirty-Seven

Damon

Once back at the garage, I headed into the office to call Wyatt. As the phone rang, I felt a pang of guilt pierce my conscience. He answered with very little enthusiasm.

"Shear Performance, this is Wyatt. How may I help you today?"

I cleared my throat. It was now or never.

"Hey Wyatt, It's Damon. From Drag Torque."

The silence in the background was deafening. I checked to see if he hung up. The numbers clicked the seconds away.

"Uh- H-Hey man, what can I do for you?" His voice was a bit giddy like a middle schooler.

I shuffled paperwork on my desk, trying to figure out the best way to broach the subject. The last thing I wanted was him thinking that I was using him, but I definitely need his help for the plan to go off without a hitch.

"Well, I was wondering how you'd like a shot at maybe

turning wrenches for a living instead of answering the phone all the time?"

"Uh, Yes Sir. I mean, Mr. Damon, I mea-"

I cut him off with a laugh, "Easy kid, I'm not going to bite your head off, and this isn't a guarantee, just an interview, ok?"

He took a deep breath of the other end of the line, "Yes, sir, I understand. Just got away from me for a minute is all."

"All good, Wyatt. Now, what time can you be here?"

"I'll get over as soon as I can, I've got someone here who can cover the phones for me for now."

I paced my office, waiting for Wyatt to show up, under the guise of an interview. My head jerked to the sound of my door opening as Noah peeked his head in.

"Man you have been jumpy as fuck lately. What's going on with you?"

I found myself fidgeting with my watch, twisting it back and forth on my wrist.

"I have someone coming in for an interview. Well, to figure out how we can get the plan off the ground." I had been friends with Noah for way too long to lie to him.

He straightened his lips and gave a brief nod. "So I suppose now would be a bad time to tell you that George is back with Jenna's car, and Garrett is on his way."

As I stood there, my face turned pale with surprise. Why was this happening at this moment? Before I could even utter a full sentence, George appeared behind Noah.

"Don't get your panties in a twist. She's fine. Garrett will be here because Don and Jenna will be here soon. I'll show them to the break room so you can hold the meeting with Wyatt."

I wiped my hand down my face in frustration.

"You know, somehow, that doesn't make me feel any better."

Thirty-Eight

Jenna

As my dad and I climbed into his truck, I couldn't help but feel a wave of remorse wash over me.

"I'm sorry," I muttered, nervously wringing my hands.

He paused, then turned the key and looked at me. "Now, why on earth would you be sorry, Gems?"

I felt ashamed, I didn't do anything to deserve what I was going through but that didn't mean that my parents deserved to go through it with me.

"You and mom are getting to know each other again and here I am with a baby raccoon who is healing from surgery, running from who knows what. Taking care of me shouldn't be your job." My tears began to stream down my cheeks before I realized I was crying. I averted my eyes.

With hesitation, he extended his aged hand towards my face and gently wiped away my tears as he had done so many times when I was a little girl. "Now, Jenna," he began softly. "I know

I've said it before, but I'll say it as many times as you need to hear it. Even though I haven't been much of a father lately, I promise to do everything in my power to keep you and Kristen safe. Although your mother may not be happy about having a raccoon in the house, both she and I share the same concern: your well-being. We understand that Osita is important to you and we see her as an extension of yourself. And baby, taking care of you is my whole job. I'll never be able to make up for losing sight of that, but I promise you do not have to apologize to me or your mother for this."

As his hand rested on my cheek, I placed mine on top and leaned in, comforted by the familiar touch. I breathed in his scent that I vaguely remembered from before booze masked it. We pulled away from the house when I finally calmed down.

* * *

We made a small detour as we pulled into the drive thru of the Dairy Godmother. He ordered us two chocolate shakes, and as we waited for them to make it e gave my knee a squeeze.

"Keep your chin up, Jenna. This is just a setback and I promise it won't be forever. Believe me, I get it kiddo, after a certain age no kid wants to be back with their parents. Unless it's visiting."

The teenager in the window handed us our shakes, dad passed me mine and pulled away.

"My point is Gems, we couldn't bear to lose you kiddo, any of us, including Damon. Let us help you."

Thirty-Nine

Damon

The door dinged, signaling the arrival of someone. Noah and I walked out to the lobby to see who showed up first, and that was when I saw her hair flip as she walked into the conference room. Being together in my garage was like being stuck in the boney grasp of Hades, as if we were Orpheus and Eurydice. It was sweet torture having her so close yet a million lightyears away. Her father was the one who led her into the conference room. It wasn't very big nor fancy, but at least it was a place we could all meet without being in my office. Not that it stopped the guys from ruining the sanctity of my office, but I didn't mind as much as I played it out.

I loved the guys. Most days.

George crossed in front of me going to talk to her or Don, and give them the update that Garrett had yet to arrive. The door chimed again, and this time Garrett came in, taking his hat off slowly as he walked toward the conference room.

After he went in, I walked closer to see what I could hear of what they were discussing. "-So what you saw was a black SUV following you to your friend's legal firm and met her co-worker as they drove by?"

"Yes." She replied softly.

"And you believe this is related to the night you got drugged?" Garrett questioned her. As my anger overtook me, I clenched my fist. She wouldn't be making this up. I know he was just doing his job but I hated the way he was acting like he didn't care about her. Even though I knew I had to tell him what I knew and what was going on, I could not do so at this moment.

The door opened again signaling the arrival of yet another person and I backed away from the conference room as Wyatt walked in. I greeted him cheerfully, knowing that this was gonna be a difficult conversation. I needed someone that Dick would never suspect.

Wyatt and I headed towards my office and I shut the door. Without hesitating, he asked, "Is everything alright?"

I nodded and replied, "Yeah, everything's fine. Why wouldn't it be?"

He looked suspiciously in the direction he'd just come, "I mean... there's a cop car out there, and I didn't think this place worked on cars for the city."

"We don't, generally, but cops do occasionally want to bring us their personal vehicles for work. We're definitely better than whoever it is they've got working down at fleet maintenance in the cop shop. Way more experienced with performance work too. Would that be a problem for you?" I sat down in my seat and indicated the chairs in front of my desk.

He sat down across from me. My office now seemed so

cramped even though it was just the two of us this weighed on me heavily.

"No, Mr. We- Damon, I'm just not used to seeing cops out front and people acting like it's no big deal. Not that I've got an issue with cops, just not used to being around them!"

No, I'm sure you weren't, working for Dick. Cops around probably meant it was a really bad day.

"Well, here it definitely isn't, we've got all kinds coming through the door," I paused, thinking about how to proceed. I went through a pretty standard series of questions for any of the new mechanics I'd look at hiring while I mulled over how to broach what I *really* needed with him.

I wanted nothing more than to be honest with him but I couldn't be. Not entirely, at least. The less he knew the better it would be for everyone.

"Well, Wyatt, based on what you're telling me, I would love to hire you on as a mechanic, but I need a favor from you. It might be too much to ask but I need the help."

He looked bewildered as he looked around, as if to say, "*From ME?!*"

"I don't really know if I can but I'll try." His answer was cautious. I didn't blame him, we didn't really know how deep this all went and what could happen.

Nodding at him, I proceeded to explain about my father's untimely demise, and how it never felt right, but we found the cause. It could be considered a faulty tie rod but we had someone come forward.

Time passed swiftly as we engaged in conversation, interrupted only by a faint knock on my door. We instinctively fell silent and shifted our focus towards the entrance. On the other side, someone hesitated briefly before finally turning the handle.

Forty

Jenna

Being questioned by the Deputy, I felt like he was questioning my sanity rather than what was happening or what had happened. I dropped my head and knew there was no way what happened today was coincidental with me getting drugged. Standing up, I shoved my chair back with a horrible scraping noise permeating the room. I lifted my head and stared into the eyes of the deputy. It all made me want to scream.

"Answer me this, do you think I'm imagining all this? Do you think I also faked being drugged?" gritting my teeth and clenching my fists, I snapped.

Dad reached for my hand and squeezed it reassuringly.

"Jenna, I'm sorry. I know you're upset. I believe you, but I have to ask, unfortunately my superiors demand I leave no stone unturned. And any little piece of information you can recall might end up being crucial to the investigation later."

Garrett stated softly.

"I understand that, but it feels like you're getting ready to call in the men with white coats. I'm not making this up, I even told you I even have a witness of them driving by!" my voice grew louder, and I pulled my hand away from my father and hit the table in front of me glaring at the deputy. "Hell, my best friend was on the phone while I tried to lose them." Garrett gave my father a glance that looked more like a warning than a sympathetic look.

"Gems... Garrett is just doing his job. He has to be this thorough to catch the bastards that are doing this to you. He's not trying to be cruel."

I was so frustrated. I wanted to cry, to scream, to do *something*. I'd never felt so powerless before, even when dealing with my dad in the depths of his alcoholism or taking care of my little sister. I forced myself to focus on my breathing and sit down, nodding for Garrett to continue his questions while dad squeezed my knee supportively.

A few minutes and what felt like one thousand questions later, I stepped out of the conference room of the shop, taking in the sounds and sights of a busy garage in full swing. I moved to Damon's office almost by instinct, my heart was skittering as I knocked and opened the door slowly, reluctant to confront the man I still had feelings for, the one I wrongly lashed out at, if not directly accused. I knew I had no right to want to thank him but it didn't feel appropriate to be in his garage and not say anything at all to him. I swallowed hard as I stood in front of him and another man I didn't know, my face heated under their scrutiny.

Damon's gaze softened just briefly before clouding over. I chewed on my lip.

"What are you doing here, Jenna?" He asked with an icy tone. I resisted the urge to sink back.

"I-I wanted to just say thanks for keeping my car here. I also wanted to say I'm sorry to take up space here, I know that every spot is valuable and having a car stuck here that you're not even working on means that there's capacity for one less and that you're in the busiest part of your season and I'm..." My eyes flitted to the other man in the room.

I willed myself to stop talking. I did *not* want to apologize for everything in front of this new guy. The unnamed man's eyes bounced between us. I could tell he was uncomfortable.

"Maybe, I should go..." The stranger hesitated.

Damon stood up, "No, I'm sure Jenna was just leaving."

Forcing a smile, I nodded understanding he didn't want to talk to me. "I... I just wanted to say thank you and I'm sorry." Turning on my heels I dashed away from his office, hot tears threatening to fall down my face.

Forty-One

Damon

What the hell was wrong with me?

Wyatt looked at me after Jenna left my doorway.

"Damn, who was *that*? Do you always have good looking girls in the garage? If so then *definitely* sign me up! I'll do my best!" His eyes lit up playfully. I inhaled deeply, just barely stopping myself from growling.

He held his hands up in a mock surrender. "I'm just kidding man, you two clearly have something going on. I wouldn't want to get in between that. Though if I can be frank you were kind of a dick."

I slumped down in my chair, and rested my face in my hand. He was right, out of line for saying so, but he was right.

There was no way I was always this much of a dick right?

I dragged a tired hand down my face. This wasn't her fault. I was letting my pain dictate my actions like some petulant child.

"So do we have a deal?" I returned, trying to get a handle on my anger.

He shook my hand and smiled. "If you'll let me turn wrenches instead of doing fucking paperwork. Added bonus I basically get to be Batman. Everyone knows, you *always* be Batman."

I shook my head, resignedly chuckling, "Sure, you can be Batman. Be the vigilante, the darkness."

Forty-Two

Jenna

I walked out to my dad who was in a bay chatting with the guys. I looked down as my feet came to a halt. I sniffled looking at my feet hoping I didn't break down completely, shuffling my feet I almost missed the shoes that came into my blurred view.

"Jenna? Hey, I thought that was you." Noah said gently.

I wiped away the tears and plastered on a faux smile.

"Yeah, it's me. I'm sorry, but I don't think I ever got your name," I replied.

He let out a soft chuckle, "It's okay, you were kinda busy. I'm Noah. I'm Damon's best friend, and the best damn engine mechanic in this shop."

It was pretty evident he was trying to cheer me up, but why did this man who had never said two words to me *want* to cheer me up. Then it dawned on me that I was standing in a garage with four men. I was in public.

Shit, Jenna, get yourself together, you look like a child.

Damon

I walked Wyatt to the door and as I said goodbye, I heard the guys laughing in the garage.

The fuck? There should be wrenches and stuff clanging. As I approached the garage I heard them laughing and tools moving and praises.

I let out a deep, guttural growl, fueled by a surging wave of unrestrained anger.

Why were they praising her?

It was our busiest time of the year, and we were on a time crunch, so I figured her dad would still be around. My eyes were drawn to her as I entered the garage. It was as if the men were bees buzzing around a piece of honeycomb.

How fucking dare they? Each and every one of them acting like she didn't rip my heart out of my fucking chest. Like it doesn't kill me that she's here now.

Noah looked over at me, and he must have sensed my rage. I looked everywhere else but them feigning a search for a tool. Slamming the toolbox lid, I turned on my heel and walked out.

The damn thing was louder than it should have been.

Once I was back to the solace of my office I swept my hand across my desk, scattering the contents across the room, I lifted my computer chair ready to chuck it at the wall. And that was when my office door was ripped open.

My eyes flashed a warning, I bared my teeth like an animal backed into a corner. Noah stood in the doorway.

"Get. Out." I seethed.

He just crossed his arms.

"Are you fuckin' done?" he asked calmly.

I threw the chair in my grasp letting a string of curses fly.

He slammed the door behind him as he crossed the room

he got in my face.

"You are acting like a spoiled child." He said with a voice of calm fury.

My fists balled in unadulterated anger at my sides and eyed him angrily.

"How dare you! *You* know that I love her!" The words that tumbled out of my mouth sounded like my voice but also like someone else speaking. I was taken back and judging by the look on Noah's face he was just as confused as I was.

"You fuckin' moron! *Noone* is trying to take her away from you, even if you're *damn* sure actin like you *want* to push her away! We're just trying to cheer her up; because when she decided to come to you with a little fucking gratitude and grace after getting grilled by Garrett, she *left* looking like she was fit to bawl her eyes out. You were the only one being unreasonable here, but that shouldn't be a fucking surprise!" He finally snapped as he screamed in my face, his saliva splattered on my face.

"You're always fucking unreasonable you fucking selfish prick! All she wanted was to spend time with you. Then she had something traumatic happen. Heaven *forbid* you were inconvenienced or made fuckin' uncomfortable."

"Fuck you," I hissed. "I thought you were supposed to be my best friend!?"

Forty-Three

Jenna

The sounds of shouting quickly faded as the sound of tools and the men getting back to work filled the air. Dad grabbed a pair of ear protection. He motioned to me to put them on and then guided me over to a different car. He handed me a wrench and pointed to a nut that looked like it had been loosened already. I twisted it loose and took it all the way off, then handed it to him.

He winked at me and mouthed "Atta girl" with a big smile.

I smiled back.

I missed this, dad and I had always been close. Well, before the drinking. It felt good to be spending time with him, even in the wake of what just happened. I felt safe in this garage full of strangers, knowing that Damon and dad were close. Damon may hate me now but I know that he'd never let anything happen to me. Especially in his garage, it was bad business.

I helped my dad mainly by handing him the wrenches he

indicated for, but soon he looked towards Damon's office and stepped towards, me motioning for me to take my headphones off. I slid them off my head and handed them to dad who tossed them gently in his tool box. He closed the distance between us and ruffled my hair the way he used to when I was a kid.

"Alright, Gem, let's get out of here. How about we grab some food on our way home?"

Ducking away playfully, I giggled. "Won't mom be pissed that we're not eating her food?"

He almost doubled over with a belly laugh I hadn't heard in years. It brought a hesitant smile to my face, recalling the countless times we used to do this when I was little. Mom never had much of a knack for cooking; her dishes were always burnt *and* undercooked.

It was a mystery to me how she managed to achieve that combination.

Consequently, whenever Dad and I had errands to run, we would invariably make a stop to grab some food. As we walked out toward the front doors we walked by Damon's door the yelling was still happening then a thwack was heard. Dad ushered me out the door quickly.

Forty-Four

Chapter 44

⟨≈⟩

Damon

He took a step back, his eyes burning through me and his lips in a tight line. His hand suddenly retracted, and before I realized what was happening, we found ourselves exchanging blows. We managed to give each other a few solid punches before he broke off and moved towards the door. It was evident that he wanted nothing more to do with the situation, but I was still consumed by anger and he'd never answered me.

I tackled him, placing him in a headlock, "We're not fucking done here. You didn't give me a fucking answer. What, are you too afraid to tell me that you all want Jenna to yourselves?"

He sputtered, "Again, you fucking jackass, no one is trying to take her away from you!"

His elbow found my ribs shortly after, causing me to reluctantly release him. I drifted away from him as we both tried to catch our breath. With a frustrated sigh, I pressed the heels of my hands into my eyes.

"I know, man. This is just… I feel like I'm crazy. I have *never* felt this way about anyone but her. Even when we were kids. I want to protect her from what she went through from her dad up until now. I want to fix everything for her, but I can't even figure out how to take down one man."

He slid over by me and patted my shoulder. The silence that lingered between was not awkward or full of tension. It wasn't too much longer before George popped his head in as he took in the destroyed office.

"The hell happened in here? You two have a lover's quarrel?" His eyes met Noah's before locking on mine.

He shook his head before turning on his heel and heading back to the garage. Noah just kind of shook his head as he also took in the state of the office.

"You sure did it this time man."

I just nodded and stood, offering him a hand up. He took it and started helping me pick up the office, while I started feeling ashamed of myself. I picked up the papers and shuffled them, attempting to organize without saying a word. Noah helped on the opposite side of the room, then George came back into the room with a broom and dust pan, fixing me with his glare before dropping the cleaning supplies on the ground in front of him.

"You know, Damon, I can't say I'm mad at ya, just disappointed. Noah, you hit this damn fool in the head or something?"

"No, George."

"Yeah, well, maybe you ought to, god knows something's gotta knock some fuckin' sense into him."

Forty-Five

Chapter 45

Jenna

Back in Dad's truck, we made our way towards the Dairy Godmother. As we pulled into the drive-thru, his phone began to ring. Chuckling, he answered, while my mom's voice came through the speaker, sounding both tender and slightly annoyed. "Where *are* you two? This little... gremlin is whining up a storm in Jenna's room."

Dad didn't even try to hide that we were getting food.

"We're picking up dinner sweetheart, so that way you don't have to cook. Sorry about the creature kickin up a fuss, we'll be home soon." He looked over at me and winked just like he used to when I was a child. I couldn't help but smile as I rolled my eyes and checked the time.

Shoot. How did I lose track of the time? Osita was on a routine, and it was well past her time to eat.

He pulled up to the speaker and ordered for him and mom

194

then looked at me, and as I ordered a patty melt he smiled.

"You never changed your order even after all these years?"

Seeing how happy this small thing made him I couldn't help but giggle.

"I usually get it, of course there are times I want a juicy burger."

His eyes widened as we pulled up to the window and he said softly, "Jenna, I want you to slide slowly onto the floor."

I wanted to question him but something in his eyes told me not to. I slowly unbuckled my seat and slid on the floor as instructed.

Just as I made it to the floor, I saw a black SUV drive up beside us in the security camera of the drive through. A teenager opened the window and took dad's card, but apart from a confused look, didn't react. I just curled myself tighter into a ball, trying to disappear completely.

Why were these men still trying to find me? I wasn't worth anything. I wasn't special...

I heard and watched the car door open, the sound of teens in the SUV filled our car.

Dad looked sheepish.

"Sorry kiddo. Um, so, less action movies, you said?"

Forty-Six

Damon

I reluctantly pulled into my garage. I'd been finding it harder and harder to come home to this place where I was stuck in my head, alone. All I wanted to do anymore was trash this place. It felt more a prison than a home. I dragged myself out of my car to the door and let out a groan.

Something has to give. I can't just trash my place, but I also can't take much more of this feeling.

I decided to start shuffling things around, like changing my bed to the guest room, hoping that would allow me to get a good night's sleep.

Though, I doubted it.

I showered in my bathroom for the last time. I had lost control of my life. I hadn't been as angry as I was today since dad's death, if even then. And over... what?

Jenna *wasn't* mine and I was the one acting like friendship was wiped off the table.

I guess I was a bigger ass than I thought I was.

As I moved the last of my clothing into the guest room closet my phone vibrated against the dresser. I sighed as I trudged over to look at the screen.

"Mom" appeared with the photo she loves of me kissing her cheek. I briefly debated on pressing ignore on the call but knowing my luck she would only call back more. Reluctantly I pressed the answer button.

"Hey Ma." I said trying to sound normal.

"Cut the crap Damon, I know what happened." She said in an accusatory tone.

Oh.

Shit, the last thing I needed was an earful about wrecking my office, but who would've told her? I dragged an exasperated hand down my face.

"What did you hear?"

She huffed. "That you and Michael got into an argument. You know he's been doing those forms for years, and I know *Greg* is a shady character *just* like his father, God love him. I know he was voted into his position, that's besides the point. Anyway, I *also* believe that *you* don't have the paperwork. I just don't understand why Michael and you can't work together like the old days? You never fought like this."

I sighed in relief. I should've known no one from the shop would have said anything about today.

That was until she heard a door shut.

"Oh dear, I am not intruding on you having a visitor, am I?" Her voice sounded almost down right giddy.

Fuck.

I hated to burst her bubble but it needed to be done before she started thinking about wedding bells and more grandkids.

"Actually, mom, no. Jenna and I have been apart for a bit, but that is not even the worst part about all this…." I proceeded to tell her everything that happened from the start, all the way through today. I don't know when it started, but, for the first time since dad's funeral, I cried.

"Mom, I- I don't know how to fix this. I think I'm going to have to move. I can't stand even being in this house. But I know that won't do any good. No matter where I live or where I am, she's all I can think about."

I heard her soft sniffles from the other-side of the line. I hated that I made her cry over me, again..

"Oh sweetheart, my baby boy… you finally let yourself find love. Who would ever have thought it would be with the same girl you loved as a child." She chuckled softly. I could almost see the memories she could see.

We talked for over an hour, planning how I was going to correct my shitty behavior.

Forty-Seven

Jenna

We made it back to my parents' without any more problems, real or imagined.

Dad kept apologizing profusely, I lost count of how many times I heard some version of, "I'm so sorry Gems, I overreacted. Just hearing the description of the SUV has me on edge, and then I saw that car roll up next to us..."

Finally, after this most recent repeat, I chuckled and patted his hand.

"I know that you were just trying to look out for me, and I really appreciate that," I laughed, "it's like old times!"

The old familiar smell of my childhood home mixed with the aroma of our food. I felt very nostalgic as I walked to the fridge and grabbed Osita's food and my blender that I brought with me from home. I blended up her food before starting on my own. Dad watched me with curiosity and warmth, while mom tried to hold back her disgust of seeing me adding the grubs to the blender.

Mom shook her head remarking, "I think she can wait to eat until you're done eating sweetheart."

I continued to make her food with a sigh.

"I can wait a few minutes, mom. It's not going to kill me to wait, I won't starve."

Mom opened her mouth to say something else, but dad not so subtly reached over and squeezed mom's hand.

"Now Amelia, she is an adult. She can make her own decisions." he told her, his voice firm, yet gentle.

She rolled her shoulders releasing the tension and huffed. "I *suppose* you're right. Did Jenna tell you what Kristen and Mark did today? *Instead* of getting a dress for the wedding we *were* planning?"

I wanted a hole to open right here in the kitchen and swallow me whole. Why was I the one that was going to get yelled at? Kristen and Mark were the ones who weren't happy with the big wedding. His eyes glanced between mom and me expecting an answer from one of us. When my phone rang. I said a silent prayer thanking anyone who was listening.

"Hello?" I answered.

"Jenna!" Kristen shrieked happily.

I pressed the speaker button, "*Hey* sis! I'm here with mom and dad! Do you wanna tell them about what happened today?"

She got quiet, and the silence was becoming more tense before Mark's voice filled the room.

"Hey Jenna, Don, and Amelia." His voice revealed that he'd rather be anywhere else than having this conversation. They should have known that they were going to be the ones to have to tell dad and everyone else, I certainly wasn't being the messenger for everyone.

I opened the door, the rest of this is them walking through it.

My dad spoke up. "Hey Mark, you uh, maybe wanna let me in on the big secret? So Amelia and Jenna can stop glaring at each other."

Kristen's voice filled the speaker softly. "Actually, dad, can we come over?"

Mom didn't even give dad a chance to respond. "You absolutely better get over here and explain yourselves."

I sighed, part of me was happy that I wasn't the one being yelled at for once.

For now, at the very least.

I took the opportunity to sneak to my room and feed Osita, whose annoyed chittering made it clear that you didn't have to speak the same language to be yelling at someone.

When I returned to eat my sandwich, mom was nowhere to be found, and dad was sitting at the table still waiting for me with half of his sandwich. I looked at his plate still on the table and raised my eyebrow.

"Hey kiddo. Just, y'know, while you're here, as long as I'm home, you won't eat alone. I hope you don't mind."

I smiled at him. I loved seeing the glimpses of the dad I once knew, and knew also that he was still fighting his demons; but I was going to keep my promise that as long as he was *trying*, putting effort towards his family, and not drinking I was going to be receptive to his efforts.

While I was taking a bite of my sandwich, he looked at me and chuckled. "So, do you want to tell me what your mom's panties in a bunch?"

I laughed. We *never* talked this candidly, and I had to giggle.

"I think it best if we wait for Kristen and Mark to explain. Mom's just hurt and upset that she has a spinster for a daughter."

This time he laughed out loud, the same belly laugh he'd had at the shop. I couldn't help but laugh along with him!

Forty-Eight

Damon

~ᘓᕘᕀᕘᘔ~

Here we were, on the first test day of the season. Everything seemed to be going smoothly for every team, except for a few minor issues like missing ten millimeter sockets, half-inch wrenches, and tire gauges. These were common occurrences, nothing out of the ordinary. Don and George approached us, accompanied by their wives, Jenna, and a raccoon in a carrier. I could only assume the raccoon was Osita. Despite my urge to go greet them, I held back, tightly gripping the wrench in my hand. My little outburst didn't seem to discourage her from looking in my direction. I could feel her blue eyes following my every move. It wasn't long before I had to step away from the car and head to the trailer to clear my mind. While I busied myself with nothing in particular, I heard footsteps approaching the trailer. I started reorganizing the tools. She stood at the entrance of the trailer with the light around her.

Fuck me, she looked like an angel with the way the sun lit

through her dress. I could hear the tiny pop as she opened her mouth to say something before closing it again.

I averted my gaze, unsure of what to say or how to proceed. Osita chirped in her carrier, breaking the tight silence, before Jenna spoke.

"Sorry- I didn't realize this is where you went. I wanted to put Osita in the shade, and this is the only place with shade."

I nodded. If I said anything at all I was afraid I was going to tell her everything that I'd been dying to tell her, all at once. I wrestled with myself for weeks to pick up the phone and just bare everything to this woman. This woman who, more than ever, I am *certain* I have loved since we were seven.

She sat Osita down and talked to her like she was a child and for a brief moment I saw her in a white dress walking down the aisle towards me, and then glowing and happy, pregnant, smiling at me. I shoved some tools into the overhead compartment and braced against it and hung my head in shame.

She must have noticed and in the softest voice I barely heard.

"I'm sorry if me being here makes you uncomfortable. Dad hardly lets me out of his sight when I am home and this was the only way to get Osita used to the outside world before I have to make a decision to have someone adopt her or release her. I am just trying to get her used to every kind of environment."

I looked at her and just knew she could see the hurt in my eyes just as I could see it etched on her face.

"Gem," I brought back what I used to call her as a child. I never realized how accurate the nickname was for her. "Kitten.

It's not uncomfortable for me, really, but I am struggling to restrain myself. I have done *nothing* but act like a jackass since that night. I'm sure you hate me and you have every right to."

She took a tentative step towards me. My gaze dropped to her pink pouty lips.

"What are you saying Damon?"

I tore my eyes from her lips and brought them back to her eyes that felt as if they could see right through me.

"I'm sorry, Jenna. I shouldn't have taken my hurt out on you, my pain. I should have been so much more understanding of what you went through. There is just so fucking much I want to tell you, Kitten, but for now I will settle for, 'I'm sorry.'" I took a step toward her and gently brushed a piece of loose hair behind her ear. Her mouth opened and closed as I held her cherub face in my hands and swiped my thumb over her bottom lip.

"Say something. please, Kitten." Her eyes darted back and forth between mine, then down at my thumb which was still brushing her lip.

"Tell me everything Damon." Her breath was unsteady as she inhaled. Our pull was stronger than the night I had found her again. I moved my lips closer to hers.

"I promise to be completely honest with you when we're completely alone. I promise I will *always* be honest with you no matter what." My lips brushed hers as I spoke, the air around us humming with electricity. I felt it zap down my spine reminding me that I wasn't the one who died, my dad was. I was still alive, still here, and losing her for the second time had made me feel like I was a shell simply going through the motions of life. I needed her in my life like I needed oxygen to breathe. I searched her eyes for a moment but instead of pushing me away like I expected she wrapped her arms around my neck and kissed me. The kiss started off gently, then I laced my fingers into her hair, deepening the kiss before I broke away. I brushed my nose along her jawline. She let out a soft whimper as my grip in her hair tightened, and I could feel my cock already straining to be let free of my jeans.

Her being so close to me again was hitting me stronger than any whiskey I ever had, and I breathed in the smell of her warm skin, then gave her a kiss along her neck, along with a gentle nip, relishing in the small gasp that left her.

I looked down at her thighs, the way she was squeezing them together, and knew that I wanted to be the one to ease that need.

I needed to do something about this. For both our sakes, clearly.

The beginnings of an idea formed deliciously in my mind and I realized I was feeling hungry. And the one thing I wanted to eat most in the world was standing in front of me, my fingers wrapped in her hair. I smirked as I dropped down to my knees, and placed a kiss at the hem of her dress and slowly lifted it to reveal more of her perfect thighs.

Forty-Nine

Jenna

I shifted slightly to ease the ache between my legs. "Damon, there are people outside." I whined. He pressed another kiss higher on my thighs, rubbing his face on me like he wasn't sure I was real. His hands brushed against my thighs.

"Then you'll just have to be quiet won't you?" He breathed as his lips skimmed across my panties, his hands slid up my inner thighs. "God, I can't wait to taste you, Kitten."

I sighed and moaned out as I bit my finger trying to keep my composure. He slid his finger into the inside of my panties, hooking his finger dragging his knuckle up and down my pussy.

"You're so wet for me Kitten, tell me did you miss me?"

I whimpered. "Fuck. Yes. I did." My head rolled back. He pressed his knuckle a bit rougher against my clit. I hissed.

"Don't look away." He said as he leaned in, biting my thigh, then kissing it.

I brought my eyes to meet his brown eyes that seemed so much darker now with lust.

"That's my girl. I wanna taste you, Kitten. Will you let me?" He brushed his nose against my aching core. I wanted him so bad I could barely stand it.

I gasped.

He bit the meat of my thigh again. "Use your words, Kitten."

"Yes. Please."

A low rumble rolled from his throat as he slipped my panties off and slid them into his pocket. He languidly ran his tongue through my slit. I bit my hand suppressing a moan as he licked again and wrapped his lips around my clit drawing it out sucking on it. My legs shook from the pleasure. He continued to lick and sucked on my clit. He then slid his tongue inside me and used his thumb to rub my clit. As his tongue pulsed in and out of me my orgasm grew closer I could feel my walls clenching around his tongue. He pulled his tongue out and slid in his fingers.

"That's it, give it to me, Kitten. Fuck you look so beautiful." His barely whispered growls were almost enough to send me over the edge, then his lips returned to my clit as his tongue flicked against, combined with his suction, my pussy milked his fingers more.

A female voice rang out from behind me.

"Oh my God, Jenna! I saw your parents outside. I was hoping you would be here too!"

I stiffened in panic and Damon pulled away, dropping the hem of my dress and his attention to my strappy sandals before standing. There was no doubt my face was flushed. I could feel the heat in my cheeks. I patted my cheeks trying to compose myself, and hoping she didn't realize what we were up to.

Her eyes flitted between us, her smile never faltering if she knew her face didn't give it away. "I am so glad you and my knuckleheaded son are getting along again." I returned her smile and chuckled. "Me too, Mrs. West."

She let out a hearty laugh. "Please call me Alison, honey. Oh! This must be our little woodland friend, hi cutiepie! What's her name?"

Mom and dad came walking in after Alison chattering. The weeks of living with my parents had shown me just how much they progressed as a couple.

"Her name is-" in the corner of the trailer, Damon caught my eye as he licked his fingers clean, lust and mischief burning in his eyes, "fuck... Osita! I mean her name is Osita. I'm sorry, I thought I saw Damon drop something heavy out of the corner of my eye."

I heard a low chuckle come from Damon's side of the trailer.

Fifty

Damon

As I stood off, I eyed my mom suspiciously. If she had seen anything, her face certainly didn't give her away.

I had to hand it to the woman, the years of raising Michael and I on her own gave her a *hell* of a poker face. I sure as shit wouldn't bet against her. I focused my attention on Donovan and his wife, I noticed that Jenna stood a bit straighter, I wiped my hands on a clean rag, reached over and gave her hand a gentle squeeze. She turned and smiled at me. I offered my other hand to her mother who quickly took it.

"I haven't seen you in ages!" She almost squealed, Jenna removed her hand out of mine so quickly.

"I have to give Osita a snack!" She damn near sprinted out of the trailer with the carrier, before I could follow her out her mom stepped in front of me again cutting me off.

"Oh she'll be back, I swear that damn raccoon is her whole life. I'm sure I don't understand her." I looked at my mom standing off to the side smiling pleasantly at us.

"Now now, Amelia." Don warned, his voice stern but gentle, she blushed and stepped closer to him. She gave an almost apologetic smile and stepped out of the way. I went after Jenna and Osita, who was climbing all over Jax like a jungle gym. I approached Jenna carefully, instead of spooking her she turned and gave me a warm smile. There was nothing more I wanted to do than throw her over my shoulder, take her to my car and have her right there in the back seat like we were a couple of teens. That said, I also wanted to do nothing but mark her so everyone knew who was the last one who made her cum.

There was a *lot* running through my mind, all of it sinful. All of it focused on *her*.

I must have had it written all over my face because I watched a flicker of that same depraved impulse spark in her blue eyes. I fought the urge, but I couldn't resist pressing my lips to hers hard in an absolutely unforgiving manner. I wanted her lips to be swollen from kisses even though it had been only a few moments since I had my mouth on her.

Selfishly, I also wanted her to taste herself on my lips. I pulled her closer to me, she wrapped her arms around my neck, her lips still pressed firm against mine. I broke our kiss and tipped her chin up towards my eyes before nipping at her bottom lip. When she gasped I slipped my tongue into her mouth. The moan that left her reverberated through me like a shockwave, I growled back in resoponse gripping her tightly and pulling her body flush with mine.

Jax spoke up with his Welsh accent. "Damon, it's almost time to go to the starting line."

She tried to take a step back away from me, I held her firm

against me, claiming her. She whimpered into my mouth. The taste was delectable.

Fifty-One

Jenna

A few hours passed and things were winding down. Since Damon's test run, he didn't leave my side for more than a couple minutes. As soon as he was able to, he was pressing a kiss to my temple and wrapping his arms around me and holding Osita's case.

Once everything was packed up and they were rolling the car into the trailer. He cornered me, pressing my back to the trailer that was warmed by the sun, his arms on either side of me, he dipped his head and talked low to me.

"Come home with me, Kitten. I want to explain what's been going on, and it has been *far* too long since I've had you on my tongue." I blushed at him, and nodded.

His hand gripped mine and pulled me to the trailer he peeked his head in and said something to Noah who looked at me and smiled. He then pulled me to his car, opening my door for me and swatting me on the butt and making me squeal as I crawled into the car. He leaned in and fastened my seatbelt for me, then pressed a lingering kiss to my lips.

"I just wanna make sure you're safe."

His brown eyes looked like melted chocolates with gold flecks in them.

I exhaled my breath slowly before giggling. His dimples came out to play as he smiled.

The drive to his house was quiet, with us just enjoying being in each other's presence. I felt him place his hand on my thigh and my mind went rushing back to the restaurant, and to the trailer, to those moments that were so intimate and yet drove me so wild even now. I felt a rush of heat flood through me at his touch. I wanted this, and I wanted him, in spite of everything we'd been through.

He carried Osita inside and put her in a guestroom with fruits, veggies, and water, then he closed her in the room. I couldn't help but feel my heartstrings being tugged at, watching him be so tender and thoughtful with her.

He turned towards me, dipping his head and giving me another kiss before tugging me back to his room.

A few feet away from the door of his bedroom he pressed me against the wall and kissed me deeply before dropping slowly to his knees.

"I haven't done many great things, but making you cum on my tongue, feeling and tasting your pleasure is by far the best thing I have ever done in my life."

I bit my lip to stop myself from moaning. He gently lifted my leg and undid one of my strappy sandals, pressing a kiss to my ankle, then working his way up my calf, slowly, agonizingly, deliciously slowly to my knee. Then sliding my sundress, inch by excruciating inch up my thighs. The licks, sucks, and bites became more fervent; I felt myself tremble with anticipation.

My head lolled back in pleasure. He nipped on my thigh and I let out a yelp of surprise and pain.

"Eyes here Kitten, if you look away again it'll stop."

He lapped at the bite mark, to soothe it. A soft whimper escaped my lips as I brought my eyes to his.

"There's my good Kitten."

He tenderly lifted my leg onto his shoulder with his large hand. His lips quickly wrapped around my clit, and with a slow suck, my knees buckled. His hand pressed against my rib cage, forcing me to stay on my feet as he continued to lick and suck on my clit.

My eyes almost closed, fuck I know I wanted to close them and lean into the pleasure, but I never looked away from him, it was just too good, and I didn't want it to end. Slowly, my knees found their strength and I was able to stand again. My hands gripped his hair, tugging gently.

Fifty-Two

Damon

I slid my free hand to her waist and ripped her panties off of her, the last barrier between me and her heavenly pussy, some back part of my brain delighting in her gasp at feeling the fabric rip against her body. My mouth salivated as I inhaled the scent of her arousal. I wanted, no, I *needed* to feel this woman as soon as possible, my cock was already throbbing for her. Her moans echoed through my hallway. I glanced up to make sure I still had her eyes on me, as I continued teasing her clit with my tongue and feeling her twitching and bucking against me. Her eyes were nearly closed, lost in her own lust and pleasure, but they held mine.

"That's my good fucking girl." I growled before giving her clit a long, slow suck.

She whimpered, giving rise to a chuckle from me.

"Damon fuck I want to taste you so bad" she moaned needily, causing my cock to twitch involuntarily.

"Please Damon, please let me suck your cock…"

That did it.

"Say no more, kitten."

With a growl I stood and swept her up in my arms in one motion, heading towards the bedroom.

She breathed out a giggle at the sudden sensation of being lifted and carried down the hall. My lips found hers while I walked, trailing kisses to her throat as I crossed the threshold into my bedroom. Her breath felt hot on my neck as she let out another whimper against me.

I tossed her onto the bed, which elicited a small squeal this time, and started to undo my pants.

"No, please," she breathed, eyeing me hungrily, "let me help…" She crawled towards me on her hands and knees to the edge of the bed, reaching toward my belt buckle with trembling hands.

She reached towards my belt with quivering hands, fumbling only a moment with the belt buckle, and breaking eye contact once again.

"Hey! Eyes. On. Me…" I reminded her forcefully as I took her chin in my hand.

"Yes, Damon…" she whimpered in reply. With that, she finally managed to free my cock from my jeans and I let her chin go as I moved my hand to the back of her head, taking her hair in my fist. She leaned in to my cock, my hand helping to guide her, and her tongue tentatively traced the outline of her lips. The late afternoon sun streaming through the blinds catching my piercings that glimmered in her blue eyes like stars.

Her tongue reached out, and swirled around my head down my shaft tracing each vein, each piercing, and my breath caught in my throat at how good she fucking felt. My cock jumped at her attention, settling back as she opened her mouth to the head, and took me deeper into her. As I went deeper into her mouth, my hand grip tightened on her hair near the scalp, tugging gently as I controlled how I fucked her face. I could feel her nails digging into my thighs to temper my speed, as my head gently pushed into her throat.

She gagged slightly but didn't try to stop me or tear her eyes from mine. I groaned. *"Fuuck*, Kitten, your mouth feels so good wrapped around my cock. Let's see how well you can take me. I wonder if you can take all of this fucking cock. Show me what a greedy little thing you can be for me."

Fifty-Three

Jenna

My head bobbed on his length, gagging slightly. He threaded his fingers into my hair, massaging my scalp as he tugged on my hair in an insistent pressure to continue the attention I was giving him. I tried to relax my throat and fight against my reflexes to take him further into me, and I could feel the pressure becoming more insistent in my hair and he began to thrust his hips in time with my strokes. My gagging intensified, and I had to pull back to take a breath. A stream of praise flowed from his lips, as my warm bridge of saliva connected me to his throbbing cock.

"You're doing so good for me, Kitten. Catch your breath, baby. I'm so proud of how deep you went, look where your lipstick is." He moaned as his rough thumb brushed against my cheek.

I moaned as I nuzzled into his hand and purred.

I can do it, I can take all of him.

My head dipped down as I tried to continue, but his grip on my hair wouldnt let me. Instead, he pulled me to his lips and kissed me.

"I love your mouth, Kitten. I don't think I can wait any longer."

His warm breath ghosted over my lips, cheeks, and down my neck. His hand lightly gripped the back of my neck. Laying me back on the bed, he settled between my legs. Taking his cock in hand he rubbed it through my folds. Before pressing it against my entrance.

"I want you to remember this for the rest of your life. Tell me you want my cock, Kitten."

My mouth fell agape as his thumb traced my lips before dipping it in and caressing my tongue before dragging his thumb over my teeth before pulling my lip down.

"Tell me you want this, Kitten. Tell me you want my cock, and you want us."

My blue eyes never leave his molten chocolate ones. One one word fell from my lips in a breathy whisper. "Yes, I want this, I want your cock, I want *you* Damon, now please…"

He lifted me with ease, my legs wrapped around his waist as he lowered me onto my back on the bed.

Fifty-Four

Damon

As her soft body pressed against me, I knew that this was the closest I would ever be to Heaven, I would do anything for the rest of my life to keep the blonde angel under me by my side. I pressed a kiss to her forehead as I dragged my cock through her wet folds pressing it to her clit for a moment, before giving her a couple sharp taps and lining myself up with her entrance. My head eased its way into her.

I let out a small gasp, which she reciprocated. spurring me to press myself deeper into her. Inch by slow inch as I felt her walls clench around me. This was a slow, sweet torture that I craved more of. Soon, I slid all the way in and held it there to acclimate to her. I slowly began to move, savoring every moment. I felt her breathing become deeper and her body trembling with pleasure.

There were no words for either of us, only the noises we made as I quickened my pace, pushing her closer and closer to the edge. Every sound she made just gave the incentive to continue until she was screaming my name from under me. I knew I said I wanted her to remember this for the rest of her life, because she was mine. Regardless of how she felt about it. She was my end all. No one would ever touch me, kiss me or have me that wasn't her.

Leaning down, I pressed my tongue flat against her sternum, licking up the thin sheen of sweat that had developed on her. I traced my lips over her collarbone, savoring the taste of her skin. I dragged my hands over her hips, feeling the curves of her form. I tightened my grip around her waist, pulling her closer. I reached down, positioning one of her legs on my shoulder, sinking deeper into her sex.

Her voice reverberated off the walls of my bedroom. Her pleasure, and my name like the most passionate prayer I'd ever heard. Our bodies moved together in perfect harmony. I kissed her neck, inhaling her scent as her hips ground into my own. Her orgasm rushed through her body, sending shockwaves of pleasure through mine. I felt her body shudder as I came, flooding her with my pleasure. I stayed, my cock throbbing deep inside her until I felt myself go limp, and I rolled off her gently, pulling her to me, peppering her face with kisses.

After our intimate encounter, we slowly succumbed to the blissful embrace of slumber.

Fifty-Five

Jenna

A few hours later I woke up to the sound of Osita's happy chirps in the next room, so I wandered in to check on her. I saw that her carrier was empty, and that at her window was another raccoon, also chittering happily. Once she realized I was in the room she scurried over to me and stood on her hind legs. I scooped her up and carried her back to the window while the other raccoon watched us.

The other raccoon pawed at the screen and Osita leaned forward to touch the window. I knew as much as I didn't want to, it was the best decision for her, and this was her sign that she was ready. I took a deep breath as I wandered through Damon's dark and silent house, opening the back door. I carried Osita out giving her praise and love as the bittersweet tears dampened my cheeks.

I let her down a few feet away from the other raccoon, keeping a watchful eye in case I needed to intervene. The raccoons sniffed and chattered at each other for a moment before scampering off. Osita stopped, looking back at me for a moment. I couldn't help the sob that tore itself from me or the tears that fell. When a pair of arms wrapped around my waist, I jumped, but recognized Damon's deep, slow breath.

He nuzzled his face into my neck, his warm breath tickling it ever so slightly. He didn't say anything right away, he just let me cry while peppering my neck with soft reassuring kisses.

"I wondered where you'd run off to. I was hoping that you hadn't run off for real, before I could tell you everything." He whispered against my neck as he squeezed me gently.

"No.." My voice was barely recognizable. I stared where the raccoons had disappeared into the night.

He pressed a kiss to my temple. "I know how hard that was for you, Kitten. But you did the *best* thing for her. Now, let's get you inside and I'll make some hot chocolate."

Before I could argue that it was May, and too warm for hot chocolate, he pulled me inside and sat me at the island. He pressed a kiss to my forehead and set forth, gathering all the ingredients for making hot chocolate.

He opened the fridge.

"Peppermint mocha or French vanilla?" He asked, smiling at me, his tattooed torso and arms lit by the fridge light.

"Hm, French vanilla?"

He nodded and again gave me his perfect smile. "My mom used to make me and my brother Michael this whenever we were upset. I promise it helps. It won't cure it, unfortunately, but it will *definitely* help."

He set the hot chocolate in front of me with a heaping glob of whipped cream on top. He sat beside me, scooting closer as he draped his arm around me. I sipped my hot chocolate as the tears still rolled down my face. He pressed a kiss to my temple and cheek.

"Kitten, listen to me. I know how hard that was to let her go, but you knew she was ready, and healed. I am *so* proud of you. For a lot of things the past couple months you have done some hard things." He stroked my hair. I felt my heart swell with love for him.

His forefinger hooked under my chin, turning my face toward him. His dark brown eyes scanned my face before settling on my lips.

"Jenna, I have to be honest with you..." He said, moving his eyes back to mine.

Fifty-Six

Damon

I swiped my thumb against her bottom lip to get her to stop chewing on it.

"Stop that Kitten. I mean being honest about what is going on." My nose nuzzled against her temple. I felt her body relax against mine.

"Okay." She sighed, a bit happier, more content. I couldn't help but smile. That was my girl.

We ended up staying awake the rest of the night talking about everything we'd learned about Richard, "Mr. T", Reuben, and her doctor co-worker. By the time we finished talking we had ended up cuddled up on my couch. The sun was coming up as the birds were chirping. She stretched and yawned, rubbing her eyes.

Before I could stop myself, it slipped out.

"I love you, Jenna."

Her blue eyes snapped open staring at me, shock, warmth

and love glimmering in her eyes.

"You do?" Her softly sleepy confused voice questioning whether or not I loved her made me happier than it should have. I smiled back at her.

"Of course I do. I should have fought harder to get you back, but after you were drugged, you needed time and as much as it hurt me, space. I was blinded by selfishness, and I don't intend to ever make that mistake ever again."

As I caressed her face she leaned into my touch and my thumb slowly brushed her bottom lip as it trembled.

Her voice was thick with emotion and cracked as she spoke. "I love you too, Damon."

That's all it took and my lips were back on hers.

I leaned her back into the couch, keeping my lips on hers, and she let out a contented sigh.

My hand slid from her cheek to her neck giving it a gentle squeeze, before ghosting over her breast and down to her hip and tugging her hips flush against mine. She ground into me as my hand reached behind her and squeezed her ass, my fingers finding and grinding against her core. Her body was trembling with pleasure and anticipation as I continued to kiss her. Our hands explored each other's bodies like it was the first time all over again, each passing second increasing my need for her and adding urgency to my exploration. She felt so fucking good to touch, was so responsive as I brought my other hand up her thigh and under the hem of her shirt, sliding her thigh to my hip, feeling the warmth of her radiating through my trembling fingers as my hand climbed higher, brushing against her supple ass.

Her hand slipped into my sweats, freeing my cock from its confines. Her soft hand stroked me to life as she gently dragged her nails down my shaft. My fingers brushed against her panties, she moaned softly. Pulling her panties aside she hissed as she stroked me, kissing me as our tongues danced lazily together. I couldn't resist touching her. My fingers dragged lazily up and down her folds before I swirled my middle finger around her clit, causing her to grind into my hand. My fingers found her entrance and slid easily into her, offering her my palm to grind against as I curved my fingers inside her.

We made out like a couple teeangers on my couch, lost in each other and reveling in every moment of it. I could tell by her grip on my cock that she wanted to come apart on my dick. I continued to stroke her g-spot as my thumb rubbed her clit. It wasn't long before she came undone on my hand.

I shifted our position on the couch, allowing us to embrace in a spooning position. She kept her face directed towards mine. With tenderness, I removed her panties, followed by sliding off my own sweatpants. Meanwhile, she pulled my shirt that she wass wearing over her head. I held her leg gently up and her small hand reached between her legs giving me a lazily stroke and teasing herself with the head of my cock before sliding the tip into her entrance. I eased myself deeper and began thrusting rhythmically into her.

Her soft moans and pants filled my ears like the sweetest music never could. We made love like that until sleep found us both, still entwined inseparably.

Fifty-Seven

Jenna

Monday morning came earlier than it should have, and Damon accompanied me to my car, well, the car that he was allowing me to borrow. He kissed me goodbye and thanked me for driving him. I drove off feeling content and happy.

That feeling dissipated pretty quickly as I walked into the building; it was like walking into a funeral parlor. Everyone was somber and the atmosphere was thick with emotion. Everyone stopped what they were doing and looked at me. I could feel the stares and whispers as I passed by.

"Amara is her office." Susan whispered as she wandered by my side.

"Oh? Wait, she's back already?" I asked.

Susan took a deep breath. "Yeah I typed that email and I meant to draft it and leave a copy of it in her office..." she trailed off.

A sigh escaped my lips as I shook my head. "Instead of saving it as a draft you sent it by accident didn't you?"

She stopped walking and looked at me sheepishly. "It's not my fault! Why do they place the draft and send buttons so close together?"

I picked up my clipboard and stethoscope, preparing to begin my rounds. All I wanted was to return to the animals who relied on me. As I did so, Susan's hand gently reached out and lowered my clipboard, her eyes fixed upon me. I looked up, meeting her eyes.

"Amara wants to see you in her office Jenna."

I caught myself just as I was about to chew on my lip, I released a sigh nodding at Susan, and headed to see what was in store for me. My gentle knock sounded at the door. Amara's rich voice echoed from the other side.

"Come in."

I hesitantly opened the door and stepped into the room where Amara was seated behind her desk, her face unreadable. She gestured to the chair opposite her, and I sat down, my heart pounding as I waited for her to speak.

"Jenna, I heard what had happened in my absence," She paused and pursed her lips. "I wanted to apologize. I am so, so deeply sorry that my soon to be ex-husband did that to you. He has since been fired."

I nodded and smiled softly at her. "Thank you Amara. I'm sorry that you had to find out through the email that Susan sent you."

Laughter bubbled up from her chest. "I have known about his ridiculous affairs for years," Her voice dropped back to her serious tone "However, I never thought that he would ever stoop so low to sell drugs."

"Wait what?" I interjected.

When I looked closer, her smile was filled with sadness.

"I didn't just get an email from Susan. I don't know who sent it but I will need to check the inventory records. I mean I had noticed a few discrepancies, like it was almost like we were being shorted by the company. I knew that couldn't be the case, at least not to the extent that we were seeing."

I nodded in acknowledgement. I wanted to know more but I wasn't about to push her for details that weren't any of my business. She seemed a bit relieved that I hadn't asked any questions about the situation.

"Amara, you know that I've been here since my first apprenticeship in college. You know how much I adore you, and the animals. I want you to get to the bottom of this."

I stood up to start my rounds for the day.

"But don't worry," I said, "I will do anything I can to help get to the bottom of it."

I gave her a wink before leaving her office.

Susan scurried over to me. "How'd it go?"

I couldn't help but laugh. "I didn't get fired. So that's a bonus."

The puzzled look on her face made me laugh harder. "Why on earth would *you* get fired?"

She followed me from enclosure to enclosure when I finally spoke up.

"I was just teasing, Susan. Seriously though, who *did* get fired?" I figured that Archer had gotten fired but I wasn't sure if anyone else had.

"Yeah Carly, and she was... *angry*." She winced slightly.

I nodded, "Yeah, well, she deserved it," I said. "It was a good lesson learned. Considering she could have lost her license."

We walked in silence until we reached our final stop, the raccoons.

Fifty-Eight

Damon

I met with Reuben and the rest of the boys to get a plan together in order to lure Richard from the shadows. Richard was powerful and we knew we had to be careful and smart to corner him. I remained uncertain about how he managed to remove tools from the other pits undetected. Nonetheless, I was convinced that he was the culprit and resolved to track him down, no matter the consequences. I was determined to end his reign of terror by stopping him once and for all.

Unfortunately that meant leaving ourselves open and vulnerable to something getting stolen or sabotaged. We had no choice, we had to act fast. We were ready for whatever came our way. We were determined. I pulled Donovan to the side.

"Are you going to tell the girls?" I asked.

"I mean I'll tell my wife. However, *you* need to tell *Jenna*."

I nodded, figuring that he was going to say exactly that. I knew he was right but I didn't want to worry her more. I knew it would be hard for her to hear, but I knew I had to tell her.

Once Don had left, I turned to Michael to go over the racing schedule for the upcoming weeks. As he laid out the plan a sense of relief washed over me. This was something that I knew, something that was comfortable.

In the meantime, we kept doing what we do best every weekend, which is racing. Every race began with me pulling Jenna into the trailer so I could devour her as my good luck charm. Once the races were done, I would take Jenna back to my home and listen to her pants, moans, and screams as I took her. Then we would get ready for the week ahead. I found solace in our weekly ritual and it kept me sane. Jenna and I became closer with each passing week.

I felt a sense of joy when I was around her and I knew that I was doing the right thing. I never wanted to lose the happiness that her presence had brought into my life. I knew that I wanted to keep her with me. I was determined to find a way to make it work for us, and I knew that I had to do whatever it took to not lose her again.

Fifty-Nine

Jenna

Since a couple weeks ago, I hadn't seen anyone following me. I still didn't understand why I was a target.

I hadn't done anything that should have gotten me followed. *Had I?*

There was so much uncertainty still, though I was at least feeling better about work. No longer did I have to worry about another animal getting hurt due to Archer's neglectful watch. The rest of the racoons were successfully released into the wild. Which... was always the outcome we wanted, even if it hurt to see them go. The pain of those goodbyes were bittersweet, and made me think of Osita. I sometimes saw raccoons around Damon's property and couldn't help but wonder if one of them was her, coming by to check up on me.

We had another race coming up this weekend and the Drag Torque team prepared to face this week's brackets which included Shear Performance which was not only a fierce competitor, but the people Damon suspected. He kept reassuring me that they had a plan but I still couldn't help being slightly apprehensive. More than slightly.

Dad and I met for dinner one night while mom had one of her social clubs that she was a part of. Dad had explained that Richard was bad news and had been since he'd raced for him. Even going so far as to tell me some things about a gambling addiction, and anger issues. Having been so young, I didn't recall him being malicious.

Either way this weekend was gonna be a lot. I couldn't shake the feeling in my gut that something terrible was gonna happen.

Emma came over to Damon's while he was working one evening, and it reminded me of how, during racing season, dad came home later too. It was nice to spend some time with my best friend again.

We talked and laughed and joked around. I felt a sense of relief at this moment, this normalcy. She sat at our island popping grapes into her mouth, complaining about Ricky, and talked about taking the leap of faith and becoming a partner at the law firm her coworker was starting. Her stream of constant chatter was a welcome presence.

"So when are you two gonna tie the knot?"

"Um- Ems we *just* got back together. Can't I enjoy the newness of this?" I said as the knife slid through the onion I was chopping.

The garage door opened and Damon walked in smiling at me and Emma.

"Smells delicious, Kitten. Hey, Emma." He said easily.

Setting down the knife in my hand I ran toward him and hopped into his arms.

"*Gross*, welp, that would be my cue to leave."

She stood and walked out the door for the evening. I sighed as I watched her leave.

"See what you did? You scared off my friend."

"Not. My. Fault. She. Scares. Easy." his words were punctuated by kisses around my face and neck, "Bye Emma! Fucking hell kitten, don't you just look good enough to eat…"

Damon pulled me closer and kissed me softly. Lifting me onto the island he moved the food out of the way and turned off the stove.

"But dinner!" I giggled.

"We'll order in. Right now, there is something else I'd rather have." He said decisively.

He carefully guided me back to prevent my head from striking the counter. Then, he removed my leggings with gentle motions and planted a tender kiss on my ankle. His lips traveled up the length of my leg, sending a shiver of pleasure through my body. His touch was delicate as his tongue carefully traced every inch of my skin, causing my body to tingle in response.

His lips finally stopped at the top of my thigh, mere inches away from my core. I let out a soft moan and pushed my hips forward just as his lips finally found their way around my clit. I closed my eyes as I felt my body shiver with pleasure and anticipation. I could feel my heart racing as his hands roamed my body.

Sixty

Damon

The long-awaited weekend arrived, and we were about to go head-to-head with Shear Performance. Tension filled the air, but despite that, everyone seemed calm and collected. We left the car unattended and gave Reuben the signal. The game cams were set up but well hidden. I had no idea if this was actually going to work or not but fuck we needed it to.

The hours wound down and once again I snuck Jenna off to take care of our pre-race ritual, opting for an unlocked storage closet we were lucky enough to find.

We arrived at the track feeling confident that the car was in perfect order. The engine hummed contentedly as I revved it up, ready to indulge in the excitement of our upcoming race. The car's paint job shimmered off the hood under the bright sun, reflecting the thrill of speed and rush of adrenaline that awaited me. It seemed like nothing could dampen our spirits on this perfect day at the track. The tires glided effortlessly over the asphalt, providing a firm grip. All of a sudden, The car lost traction, and my stomach plummeted as I realized something was wrong. As I hit the wall, all I heard was the crunching of metal and bone. The world started fading to black around me.

I knew that this was a possibility when trying to get him to sabotage our car, but this couldn't be the end of Jenna and me, not when I just got her back. I wondered what had crossed my dad's mind. The world went black before I could think any more about it.

Sixty-One

Jenna

⁓⁓⁓

We watched in horror as he crashed, and Damon's mom and I held each other while the guys and paramedics pulled him from the completely destroyed car. We knew the situation was serious, but we had to remain hopeful. We all held our breath as we waited, praying that he would be alright.

* * *

The waiting room felt like it was getting smaller, blanketing our group in a heavy silence that made us all feel powerless. We were all filled with fear, sitting there tense and trembling in the oppressive glow of fluorescent hospital lights, clinging to hope and wishing for a miracle to happen.

Finally a doctor came out and told us that Damon had pulled through, and that his mom and Michael could go back to see him. We all let out a collective sigh of relief and thanked the doctor for his good news. I couldn't move even when his mother came over to me and held her hand out to me to follow them to the room. I stood up and followed her, my heart pounding in my chest, racing faster than Damon had ever driven. As we entered the room, Damon lay in the hospital bed, cast over his arm and bandages wrapped around different parts of his beautiful body. It was so hard to see him like this, but he was breathing. Breathing slowly, but steadily and easily, with his eyes shut. The most important thing was that he was alive. Relief flooded through me and I felt my knees go weak as I collapsed into the chair in the room.

* * *

Later that night, after everyone had left and his mom had convinced them to let me stay with him. I shifted in the uncomfortable chair when I heard a groan come from the bed. I perked up and looked at him. His eyes opened groggily and smiled at me as I rushed over to him. I grasped his hand and squeezed it gently.

He whispered, "I'm okay, Kitten." I smiled back, tears streaming down my face.

I kissed him on the forehead and whispered back, "I'm so glad you're alive."

"It would take a lot more than that little fender bender to get me out of your life. You're stuck with me, Kitten."

Sixty-Two

Damon

They kept me for a few days for observation. I had managed to walk away with a few broken bones but nothing life threatening. Jenna was in the hospital every single day I was there, by my side and doing at least as much to help me as those nurses ever did. Reuben showed up one morning before Jenna had even arrived, he had managed to catch Richard messing with our car by going in with a piece of a hacksaw to cut at something on the driver's side, the back of the brake pedal being found cut through showed that his intent was to make me unable to stop at the end of the race. He slipped into the car after the qualifying times while we had stepped away. As painful as the result was, it was exactly what we needed.

Unfortunately, the damage to the car was extensive, and it would take a while to repair, but we had the evidence needed to nail that fucker to the wall. Jenna showed up and I sent Reuben on his way. Richard, the dick, could wait. We knew he wasn't going anywhere, and there would be time enough later to deal with him as we saw fit.

Throughout it all, Jenna's unwavering support helped keep my spirits up during the recovery process. I knew that I couldn't be stupid this time and let her slip through my hands again. I mean for fuck's sake, I had been *very* lucky, the wreck could have been much worse.

I was reminded of that over and over again over the following weeks. Jenna had taken the opportunity to come and fuss over me day and night. I may have bitched and moaned a little, but really, I was truly grateful for the care she gave me. Don't really know how I'd have fed myself those first few days especially, still goofy on pain meds and only having one arm to work with. She caught me trying to make myself a PB and J and watched me pitifully for a few seconds before coming and shooing me back to the kitchen counter while she took over. From then on she turned on the "domestic goddess" mode and I don't think I ever ate so well or often before.

"You're going to make me fat," I said, around a mouthful of pork roast and mashed potatoes.

"You need your strength to heal. I can't knit your bones together for you, but I can help make sure you get all you need and get the *rest* to go along with it."

"I don't need *rest*. That fucker is still out there and I need to make him pay for what he did to my dad. For what he did to my *car*."

"For what he did to you?"

I shrugged. "I'm less worried about that, I get being competitive, and I'm alive after all. Look, I'm just saying you can swing on me, but you don't touch another man's car, that's a sacred rule."

I thought I heard the sound of her eyes rolling, but I couldn't be sure.

"Sure babe, but he's going to pay for all of it. Including touching your *precious* (did that sound like "stupid" to anyone else? Just me? Weird.) car. You've got your team getting everything together, right?"

"Yeah, Reuben's got the footage, and we're putting together what we've found. I really don't want to go to the cops with this. He's right there, smug and thinking he's got us by the balls." I started to push my plate away when I caught Jenna's eye, which flicked down to the unfinished plate before coming back to me. I sheepishly took one more forkful of roast and potato before she gave a small nod and cleared the plate away.

"Anyway, I know you don't want to go to the police, and I get it, but you can't solve *all* your problems with a sledgehammer."

"I usually use a wrench, but point taken, Kitten."

"Let the cops do what they need to do. Let *justice* happen. Then everyone will know what happened back then, and he'll be rotting behind bars while you live your life." She gave my good arm a small squeeze and kissed my cheek. I wrapped my arm around her waist and let my hand rest on her hip while I pressed my head into the softness of her chest.

"I love you baby. I don't know what I did to deserve you, but whatever it is, I'm glad I did it. You're right, I just don't like that you're right."

"You spend enough time with me, Crash, and you'll get used to it."

I moved my hand to pinch her ass in response, getting a sharp yelp and a swat for my efforts.

Sixty-Three

Jenna

I thought helping animals heal was a struggle, clearly that was a lie because I had never had to take care of a man who was bound and determined to do anything and absolutely everything the doctor had forbidden him to do.

"Kitten, it's just engine work, I can't even hurt myself doing that."

I wondered if he could see my eye twitching. I was beginning to wonder if he was trying to make it twitch, because he was so good at it.

Maybe there was some improvement though, as this was the fifth time today he'd tried to sneak out to the garage, but we had fifteen escape attempts yesterday. And it had originally started with him wanting to get the tires off. I had to explain to him in *very* small words that he would *not* be able to change tires with one arm and four intact ribs. Noah *and* the boys from the shop came around *along with* his brother, sister in law and niece, but even that didn't seem to be enough to convince him that he needed rest.

"Now sweetie, can you say, 'Uncle Damon is a big dumb dumb who should listen to his lovely girlfriend instead of trying to kill himself because he's bored in the house'?" his brother said to the baby bouncing in his arms.

She burbled happily in response, and Michael nodded excitedly.

"That's right sweetie! Good job!"

"Caroline, can you tell my brother, your father, that he's a giant fuc-"

"Woah!"

"Language! Damon! I am shocked at you!" Noah and the other boys from the shop huddled protectively around Caroline who looked up at her scruffy uncles and tried to grab their offered (freshly scrubbed) fingers. "Trying to corrupt your sweet niece with that kind of filthy talk. She's gonna call you Uncle Potty Mouth when she gets big, mark my words."

"I hate all of you, individually and as a group. Except her," he grumbled, pointing to Caroline with his good hand.

I immediately put on my absolute *best* pout.

"All of us, Damon?" I whined, giving him a long slow blink as I watched him nearly short circuit.

"Kitten, no- n-"

"No, no, Damon, you said what you said and I'm sure you meant every word." I turned on my heel and quickly left the room, mostly so he wouldn't see me crack a smile at him being caught so off guard. I figured this might be the easiest way to reset his brain to listen to sanity and stay out of the damn garage and stop trying to mess with that stupid car. A couple moments later I heard a pained groan coming from

246

the direction of where I'd left him with his niece, followed by some shuffling down the hall to me.

"Mmmf... fuck, babe? Kitt- ow, goddamnit. Baby come back, please. These ow, these fucking ribs..."

"LANGUAGE! The fuck is wrong with you?" Noah yelled quietly. I put my hand to my mouth to stifle a giggle, and that's how Damon found me.

"Kitten, oh my god what have I done?" His face fell as his eyes searched mine. I couldn't help but burst out laughing. I heard him mutter, "oh, you fucking bitch" under his breath which caused me to laugh even harder.

"Language, Damon..." I said as his lips found mine.

After everyone left, I was alone with him once more.

"Damon, please," I pleaded, "just listen to the doctor and rest. You're not helping anyone by trying to push yourself like this."

"I know baby... I just, I feel so fucking *useless* right now. And that prick is still out there, doing fuck knows what and thinking he got away with it while I've got to just sit on my *FUCKING* hands because my ribs hurt a little." He winced as he took a deep breath.

"I know, but you need to give yourself the time to heal, and you need to trust your guys to get the evidence put together. Also you have broken ribs, they don't just '*hurt.*' You're not going to be any good to anyone, especially your Dad if you get hurt even worse."

Sixty-Four

Damon

A month later and I was still on the mend, but at least it didn't hurt to just breathe. Jenna was finally able to convince me to stay out of the garage, and put my trust in my team.

My guys.

They'd been with me through thick and thin, some since childhood, and all had known my father and then me when I showed up. They knew the stakes at play here, what it meant to me, to all of us. And my *god* did they fucking come through. Reuben compiled all the footage from the cam at the track, as well as any other evidence that he had lined up from the years, all pointing straight at that fucking Dick from Shear. I gathered the team together and we went through everything before calling up Garrett to give him what we'd found.

"Holy shit... this is solid. Reuben, you're willing to testify to all this, right?" He turned from the pile of papers and laptop to look searchingly at him.

"As long as I'm still around." He said with a ragged breath. "The docs have moved up my timeline, treatment hasn't been going well, they're saying I'm 'not responsive.' Wife always said I was a stubborn bastard, guess that includes this shit too."

I put my hand on his shoulder. "How long are they saying you got?"

"Well, originally they said two to four years. Now…" He got a far off look, silent for a moment before speaking again with a sigh, "maybe six months, a year at most. I'm glad I came to you when I did, Damon. I just hope I'm around to see it through."

"Me too old man, me too."

"I'm going to bring this before a judge as soon as I can. We'll have to do some investigating of our own, but guys, I think we've got him. Damon if we play our cards right, we'll be able to put this fucker away for a long time. There's dozens of cars that he's sabotaged here, if we can get even one more person from the shop to crack, that corroborates all this evidence. Well done Reuben, and thank you for finally finding the courage to step forward."

* * *

A few months later we were sitting in the courtroom, in the gallery on the prosecutor's side. It dawned on me that this was the first time I had even been on this side of the law. I was seated, my knee bouncing and my hand squeezing Jenna's for support. This was it. On my other side sat Reuben's wife, seeing through to completion what her late husband would miss.

Reuben died shortly after delivering his testimony at the

trial, from his hospice bed at home. The look on Reuben's face when Dick couldn't contain his outburst screaming at the screen "You son of a bitch! I should have killed *you* when I had the chance!" was absolutely fucking priceless. Dick's lawyer's face drained of color, and he grabbed his client, whispering urgently in his ear. The rest of the trial was pretty much forgettable after that, apart from Reuben's passing a few days later.

Shockingly, no one from Shear was there at the funeral, even the ones who weren't arrested at the time. Everyone from *our* shop was there, and so were a lot of the folks from the track. Reuben had touched a lot of lives in a lot of ways, and his part in getting rid of the cancer that was Dick Shear helped make sure that everyone would remember him in a good light. I hoped that he and my Dad were watching from wherever they were to see this bastard brought to justice at last.

Everything had come down to this final moment. The room was tense as the judge read the verdict. The man who had caused so much pain and destruction was finally going to face justice. As the gavel struck, a sense of relief and triumph washed over us. Justice had been served.

On our way home Jenna squeezed my hand looking at me with a small smile. "Reuben and your dad would be proud of you. For what it's worth I am also proud of you."

I smiled back at my girl, grateful to be closing that dark chapter of my life, starting a new one with this gorgeous girl by my side.

The End.

Sixty-Five

Epilogue:

Jenna

A few months later we were sitting around the dinner table at my parents' house. Kristen and Mark had their elopement, and had just gotten back from their honeymoon in New Zealand, both his mother and ours were not... overly thrilled that they had missed the wedding but at the end of the day they were both just happy that Kristen and Mark were happy. Dad was six months away from his first year of being sober, and his eyes were clear and bright. He and mom were working on rebuilding what they had all those years ago, and I don't think he let a day go by that he didn't thank her in some way for sticking with him through everything. I'm not sure if it was part of his Step 9, but he made sure that she knew every day that he was a changed man, and I think she was starting to see it herself. I think we all knew that it would be a long road to travel, but it was so nice having him back in our lives in such a real and present way.

Damon was keeping him around the shop, and I think between that and the support of his group, it was helping to alleviate all the guilt and tension that he'd carried with him since Miles' death.

For her part, Mom was meeting with a local Al-Anon group, and had started seeing a therapist that they had recommended. Between the two, they helped to give her a sense of community and solidarity to do what she felt was best, and she decided to keep the old man around to lavish her with the love and affection he'd been too lost to provide.

Everything was falling into place, Damon asked me to move in with him but had us meet with a builder the day I said yes, so that we could "have our dream home." We left after having dinner and dessert with my family, and once in the car we had only just made it down the driveway before he slipped his hand onto my thigh. I interlaced my fingers with his, and he held my hand while he shifted through the gears.

"How about we go and see the progress on the house?" He asked almost sheepishly.

"Sure, are you nervous I'm not gonna like it? I did help design it after all."

"Um, well, maybe. I guess. It's a big thing, you know. I have to make sure that everything is perfect for my Kitten."

I couldn't help but chuckle, he seemed to be sweating bullets and had been since this morning. All through dinner he and my dad had snuck out of the room, many times. I figured it was to hang out in the garage to get away from all the girl talk but it didn't make sense that Mark didn't go with them; though from what Kristen has said he hasn't left her side longer than a shift at work since they said "I do."

"It's sweet for you to be so worried about me, but I'm sure I'm going to love it. We've done all of this together, of course it's going to be perfect."

He smiled and brought our hands up to his lips and kissed the back of mine.

"I love you, Kitten."

"I love you too, Crash."

The car seemed to drive itself as we continued to talk about everything and nothing, before I realized that we were currently sitting in the house's driveway. *Our* driveway, I guess I should get used to calling it that. It was hard to believe that something so concrete was going to be shared with someone like Damon, the bad boy of the track who never saw himself settling down.

Damon got out of the car smoothly, and came round to my side to open my door for me. I took his offered hand and checked him out in the moonlight before getting out of the car. His hand moved to the small of my back and I leant my head against his arm while we walked.

"Well, baby, you ready to see what we've created?" He said as he kissed the top of my head.

"I think so. God why do I feel so nervous?" I asked with a giggle. I felt his lips curl into a smile.

"I know what you mean, Kitten. Shall we?"

I took a deep, steadying breath. "Let's go on in."

He took a set of keys out of his pocket and moved to unlock the door.

"Let's get a good look at your new home, Kitten."

It was perfect! Well, empty, since we hadn't brought over our furniture or picked out new, but still. I could see us in this house, our design choices blended seemlessly throughout, but what Damon said nagged at me, and I asked him as we walked into the master bedroom, our footsteps echoing off the tall ceilings in the empty space.

"This is amazing Damon, but what did you mean, *my home?* Are you moving someplace? Did Nikki steal you from me after all?"

He looked puzzled for a moment before scoffing, "Oh, god her... no baby, you're the only one for me."

"Ha, sure! I bet you say that to all the girls you build a house with."

He turned me away from the window, where I'd been looking out at the moon over the mountains in the distance. His hand found my chin and guided me to look up into his eyes, and I had to fight the whimper that involuntarily rose in my throat.

"I mean it Kitten. You asked me why I said this was your home, and the answer is simple, 'because it is.' This is your home, and baby, you're mine. I don't care if I'm living out of a cardboard box as long as I'm with you, *you* are *my* home kitten. You are the one person who's made me feel as alive as racing does, the one person I want to race towards every day," he got down on his knee, "Kitten, Jenna, I want nothing more than to spend every day of my life coming home to you, to have you waiting for me at the end of the track."

He opened a small box and an simple, elegant diamond ring sparkled inside, a platinum band with a large central diamond flanked by three smaller ones. I'd spent hours looking at rings just like that one, and I have no idea how he'd figured that out.

"Jenna, my love, and my home, will you marry me?"

It took all of 2.5 seconds for my eyes to fill with tears and me pouncing on him with a squeal and kissing him over and over again, after a minute or two of a shared kiss he pulled away looking me in the eyes, somewhere between scared and amused.

"So, is that a yes?"

"Uhm.. Yes! What kind of question is that?"

"Listen, I have been freaking out all day, and especially at dinner that you'd say 'no.'"

"I didn't know little ole me made the big bad boy so nervous" I said with a smirk.

He smirked right back at me, a fire in his eyes.

"Oh kitten, that was just pre-race jitters. You don't make me *that* nervous, I promise. Besides," his hand found the back of my head and gripped my hair near the scalp, pulling it tight and using it to pull my face up to meet his, and this time I didn't fight back the whimper, "I know *exactly* how to get you to purr for me. But this question was a little more important than where you want to eat tonight, or what color you want the bathroom to be, isn't it?"

I felt a flood of heat to my core as I looked into his hungry eyes and tried to nod, my mouth not able to form the words.

"No no, I want you to say it. Use your words for me baby, go on." his voice was dark and deep with lust.

"Yes, fuck, yes Damon." I panted.

"That's my good fucking girl." he growled, his hand moving from my hair to my throat and guiding us against the wall. His lips found mine and pressed into them in a deep claiming kiss, then he pulled back so that our lips were nearly touching "My good fucking bride to be. I cannot wait to have you in every room in this house, but I want you here, now."

He turned my head to the side to give himself better access to my throat for his hot mouth, and my trembling hands immediately went for the buckle on his belt, fumbling as I felt his tongue and teeth against my skin. I palmed his growing erection as his hand found my breast and squeezed until I gasped.

"Fuck I want you too Damon, I want you inside me." I said breathlessly, his hands and mouth creating a familiar ache in my core that needed release. I wanted him. I *needed* him, to feel full and to take control and to- his hand slipped under my dress and I felt him smile against my throat, his scruff scratching against my skin.

"No panties, kitten? Such a naughty fucking girl you are."

"I wanted to sur-ohmygod- surprise you later, I didn't think it would be here though." I said with a giggle. It was hard to think like this, my mind was clouded by the feelings racing through me with every pump of my pounding heart.

"Wait, Damon, the ring?"

He paused and looked me in the eye, confused, "What about it?"

"Put it on me, silly?" I felt his cock twitch against my thigh, and it was everything I could do not to imagine how it would feel to have his piercings slowly entering me inch by delicious inch.

"Oh fuck, right." He took the ring out of the box and I saw that his hands were trembling too, whether from lust or nerves was anyone's guess and I didn't care, but he took a deep breath, and carefully slipped it over my finger.

My breath hitched. It sparkled in the light from the moon and the room as we both looked at it.

"It's beautiful Damon, I love it."

"It doesn't hold a candle to you kitten. I'm glad you love it." His lips found mine again as his fingers slipped up my thighs to find my core, sending a shock of pleasure through me. I wrapped my fingers in his hair and squeezed as the intensity grew.

"That's very swee-fuck-sweet Damon, but I need you inside me."

Despite my words I gave a little moan of protest as his fingers left me and he stepped back and took all of me in with that hungry look in his eyes. I was beginning to understand how a rabbit felt being sized up by a wolf, and I loved every bit of that feeling.

"Dress off. *Now.*" The desire and lust in his voice did not help the trapped bunny feeling, but I decided to tease him just a little longer.

I turned around to face the wall, slipping one shoulder and then the other out of my dress, then reached back to unclasp my bra, letting the band go slack but holding it in place over my breasts. I looked over my shoulder at Damon, his hand giving his cock slow strokes while he watched, his focus completely on me and what I was doing. My dress was caught on the curve of my hips as I slowly turned around to face him again, letting the dress slink to the floor as I did so.

"You're a little fucking tease, you know that, right?"

"And you love it." I said while pulling the bra away from my chest and throwing it at him.

It had barely had time to hit him before his hands were on me, and he was kissing everywhere, his mouth hot against my sensitive skin. I felt a sharp pinch on my nipple and let out a gasp.

"What was that for?" I asked with a whine.

"For being a little fucking tease, and also because I wanted to." His tongue flicked across the pebbled skin as he finished speaking, and he dropped to his knees as he kissed down my stomach and hooked one leg over his shoulder.

"I am looking forward to spending every day devouring your delicious little pussy, kitten. I need to feel you writhing on my tongue before I fuck you." His lips clamped around my clit and I gripped the back of his head as electricity ripped through me, his tongue teasing while I felt him squeezing my ass and hooking around my other leg.

"What are you do-" I felt him stand with me on his shoulders, his tongue never stopping. The wall was cool against my back as I leaned against it, my pussy grinding against Damon, and I felt his grip sure and strong against me, his grip like iron.

I could feel the pressure building, threatening to explode out of me as I gripped his hair even tighter, moaning his name over and over like a prayer. His tongue became ever more intense as a wave of pleasure broke and crashed through me, my body convulsing against the wall and his mouth.

He lowered me gently, taking my weight on his elbows as we found our lips, tasting myself on him, our tongues dancing with each other as his cock found my entrance and pushed inside. I felt his piercings against me, felt him filling me so completely and I lost myself in the feeling, everything stirring and mingling until we were one and wholly mixed with each other.

"Fuck, that's it Kitten, you're taking me so fucking good, aren't you? My good fucking girl, making my cock feel so good in this delicious little cunt."

"YES Damon, god yes, you feel so fucking good, I need you."

I felt him growing harder inside me, his long slow thrusts increasing their intensity and speed, I felt another peak approaching as he growled in my ear, "Jenna, I'm going to fill this pretty pussy with me, I want you to come with me baby. I want to feel you come around my cock while I breed you, can you do that for me, baby?"

"Yes," I whimpered, over and over again while he thrust into me, the pressure becoming wonderfully unbearable, "come inside me Damon, fill me with all of you, please."

He growled back in reply and I came undone around him once again as I felt him throbbing deep inside me. He dropped to his knees as he pressed into the wall with me.

I felt him twitching inside me still as he kissed me, breathless.

"I love you so fucking much, Kitten," he panted, moving his arms gently to wrap around me as I finally felt him begin to soften inside me. I lay my head against his shoulder and kissed his neck, feeling him twitch once more and I giggled at the feeling.

"I love you too Damon." We stayed wrapped in each other's arms, lost in the thoughts of the past, and of our shared future.

About the Author

Natalie Ophelia Rhodes is a Mental Health Professional who specializes in holistic medical approaches as well as traditional therapy, an ordained minister for LGBTQ+ weddings, and a writer. She lives on the East Coast of the United States with her two pups, Remington and Beretta. She is a survivor, an author, and understands the importance of rising above and out of a bad situation. She is the Author of Wild Quarter Mile, Burning Embers, Rugby Anthology, and more.

Made in the USA
Monee, IL
31 May 2025

18426425R00154